The Law is an Ass

With compliments
[illegible]

The Law is an Ass

A Collection of Short Stories

by

Niran Adedokun

PRIMA

ISBN: 978-978-58491-4-1

Published in Nigeria in 2021 by Narrative Landscape Press
under its Prima imprint
9, Odunlami Street, Anthony Village, Lagos, Nigeria
07014522083, 09090554406 – 7
contact@narrativelandscape.com
www.narrativelandscape.com

A catalogue record for this book is available from
the National Library of Nigeria.

Cover Design and Text Layout by Ayebabeledaipre Sokari
Author's Photography by Tosin Ajayi

Printed and bound in India by
Manipal Technologies Limited, Manipal

To family, the very testament of His grace.

Contents

I

From Dubai With Love

For the third time in five minutes, Ladi furiously searched his pocket for his phone. It was now 11.15 a.m. He let out a prolonged hiss, wondering why he thought time had gone much further than the last time he checked.

"Why is it that time drags on when you're in a hurry?" he muttered, peeping through the window to see if Rasaki, the taxi driver he hired on occasions like this, was anywhere in sight. He let out another hiss of disappointment, seeing there was still no sign of him. This really infuriated him. *What option does a choiceless man have?* he thought, sinking into the couch which doubled as his bed at night. *But for the heavy downpour that brings chicks and doves under a shelter, what would bring me near a nitwit and destitute like Rasaki?*

"They say that when life throws you lemons, you make lemonade," he said, standing up to look out again. Rasaki was still nowhere in sight.

He had lived in the one-room flat with his wife since the serial misfortune that hit them within twelve months in 2012. In the past few months, life had started to become a bit rosier for him and Remi, his wife of five years. Before his lucky run into Adams – his old benefactor and schoolmate – seven months before, they had been living in hell. Theirs was one of the numerous stories of young Nigerians who had moved from hope into the dungeon of despair within blinkers.

Life did not start on a rosy note for this first-class graduate of Economics from Nigeria's premier university, University of Ibadan. Born into the family of Alamu, a palm-wine tapper who drank more wine than he sold, Oladipo Alamu was delivered unto the ugly laps of poverty. It was only during his days at UI, as the University of Ibadan is called, that Ladi had the first taste of the comfort that wealth could bring. Then, he would joke with Adams, his friend from a well-heeled background, that poverty lived in his own home.

Ladi and his sister, Amope, did not know the luxury of a three-square meal. Their mother, Asake, catered to all their needs from the sale of firewood to families within and around their community. The proceeds were barely enough to feed the family, but even when they lacked food, the poor lady was committed to the education of her children. Asake had seen how much education changed the lives of some families in their village and was committed to seeing her two children attain the highest level of education possible. This was without regard to the uselessness of her drunk husband who seemed to have given up on the hope of a better life.

Ladi and Amope did well in school and this encouraged their mother. Asake was one of those mothers who the Yoruba describe as *abiyamo tooto,* an exemplar of true motherhood, one who gave her all to the attainment of her children.

But sometimes, no matter what you do, life just gets the better of you. While Ladi focussed on his academics, his sister drew the opposite gender to herself like sugar draws ants. Having grown into a plump, mature beauty with full breasts and a curvaceous body, she succumbed to the hype of her own allure, sneaking out of school into the homes of men by age fourteen. By fifteen, Amope was pregnant.

The news shredded the heart of the family. Ladi who was awaiting the result of his school certificate was distraught, as was their mother. This was worsened by the fact that she could not identify the man responsible for her pregnancy. She eventually settled for Alade, an irresponsible husband of two other women. Alade would hear nothing of the pregnancy. He swore that not even death would make him accept the pregnancy.

The family fought this war throughout the nine months of Amope's pregnancy. Unfortunately, she lost her life to excessive bleeding two hours after she was delivered of a baby boy. Two days later, the new-born trailed behind his mother in the premature journey to the world beyond.

Mama Ladi watched helplessly as she lost both her daughter and grandchild within a few days. It was the day she stopped living. A few months after, she came down with a strange illness which she never recovered from, waking up at midnight with complaints of a severe headache. It was too dark to embark on the fifteen-minute journey to the dispensary in the next village, so, she drank the all-purpose concoction of herbs on the ceiling of their thatched-roof home and that sent her to sleep until daybreak.

By the time he checked on his mother in the morning, her eyes were wide open but she neither spoke nor responded to anything said to her. Death snuffed life out of her before they could get her to the dispensary, and an era ended.

Ladi moved in with his mother's only brother. He took a labourer's job at the construction site of a fuel station, while awaiting the results of his school certificate examinations. Two months after, the results were released. He made the best result in the whole region and was offered a scholarship which covered the tuition to study Economics at the University of Ibadan. It was news that left a sweet and sour taste in his mouth as he wondered how glorious it would have been for his mother to witness this beautiful day. But life had to go on. He proceeded to the University of Ibadan.

Once again, Ladi shone like an isolated star at UI. He studied ahead of classes, such that when lecturers, in the conceit of their superiority, brought challenges, he was almost ever ready. While other students misused their time, Ladi never lost his head. He always reminded himself that he was in school to study and made only a few friends.

One of his very few friends was Adams, the third son of a retired general. Unlike most other rich boys on campus however, two things stood Adams out – his willingness to learn and his unusual generosity. A combination of these factors drew Ladi to Adams and the two of them soon became inseparable. It was a mutually beneficial relationship that looked like a match made in heaven.

Ladi helped his friend overcome his academic weaknesses while Adams made sure that his indigent friend lacked nothing. For the first time in his life, Ladi rode in the front seat of a vehicle owned by someone he knew, he learned to dress like a gentleman and ate a number of things he never thought he would taste in his lifetime.

He jumped up from his reverie when he heard the engine of Rasaki's rickety Mercedes Benz 200. He picked up his phone to see that a clear thirty minutes had crawled by, searched for the key to his apartment and dashed out to start the forty-five-minute drive to his Isolo destination.

After giving the driver a piece of his mind for the delay, Ladi opened the front door of the car and sank into the passenger's seat. Rasaki put the car in motion without saying a word. It was three minutes into the trip when Ladi noticed that the air-conditioning in the car was off.

He yelled, "Ogbeni, why is this AC not on?"

The driver started in a shaky voice. "Na only as I dey come..."

"Abeg, leave that matter," Ladi interrupted. "This is what you always do but I don't blame you. I don't even know why I still call you to take me out. None of this is your fault, just keep quiet abeg!" He raved at an already subdued Rasaki.

As much as I would love to forget all my life's troubles, foolish people like this Rasaki won't let you be in peace. Anyway, all of this will soon end, and I will be able to do everything that I want to do again. Life cannot keep being so unfair to me.

Although Ladi had had some hard moments, one couldn't really say that life had been totally unfair to him. After the loss of his mother, he got more than a friend in Adams. The son of the general stood with him, making sure he lacked nothing, such that Ladi almost forgot the misery of his past and came out at the top of his class.

He got an offer to teach and start his post-graduate degree at the Department of Economics where he graduated, but decided to take up an appointment with a banking institution which offered good money and a better career opportunity. "Teachers, whether they are lecturers or not, are always poor people and I think I have seen enough poverty for one lifetime," he told his friends.

He was recruited by the bank and deployed to the Business Service unit where he once again excelled. Within five years, he became an assistant manager because of his contribution to the department and bank's growth. Within these five years, he married Remi, whom he started dating during his final year in university.

Remi was an excellent Christian girl whose time was divided between classes, church and the library. At the beginning Adams, teased that Ladi had no chance with this *spiricoco* who had no social life, but he underestimated his friend's tenacity. Ladi was prepared to do anything to win the heart of the elegant and god-fearing lady, including tagging along to her religious events. Even then, Remi rejected his advances for another year, and it was not until his final year that the wall of her resistance crumbled.

With his influence in the bank, Ladi got his beau a job in one of the branches. She however had to quit when they got married two years later, since the bank policy was against employees being married to one another. Remi also desired to have her own retail clothing business instead of a bank job. She often complained about the stress she experienced as a marketer and how investing time in a private business would ultimately benefit the family.

By the time they were married, she no longer had to worry about convincing Ladi. In his private moments, he had also ruminated over the need for some measure of flexibility for his wife, especially as they were soon going to start having children.

When they travelled to the United Arab Emirates for their honeymoon, half the time was spent scouting for business opportunities for the new bride. After sealing a couple of deals, they agreed that Remi would return to Dubai after arrangements for a suitable location for the boutique would have been made.

But this was not to happen. Two weeks after their return, the new Central Bank governor announced that four of the country's fifteen banks were in a precarious position. He also announced the withdrawal of the licences and nationalisation of the banks, while emphasising that those perceived to have run the banks poorly would face the music.

The Central Bank went on to issue licences for four bridge banks, established to acquire all assets and liabilities of the solvent banks until such a time that the Deposit Insurance Company would find suitable investors willing to acquire the banks. This was the beginning of the crash of Ladi's hopes.

Things happened quickly within two months of the takeover of the bank where he worked. The managing director/founder of the bank was arrested alongside all his executive directors, and a new management appointed by the Central Bank summarily dismissed the rest of the management staff.

Ladi saw his life crumbling down like a poorly constructed wall. Having committed his entire life to his job at the bank, he had no plans for the rainy day. The only investment he ever thought of was the one Remi had been about to embark on, which could no longer be because he lost his job.

When his friends were investing in landed property and stocks, Ladi saw no need for it. To him, life was good, and as long as he could work and earn a salary, there would be nothing to worry about. On a few occasions, he had told his investment-crazy friends that they were not so smart after all. One of those occasions was when a lull hit the stock market months after he was goaded to buy 200,000 units from his bank's Initial Public Offer.

Most of his salary and allowances had gone into looking good and maintaining friends in the elite class. He lived the life of a top bank staff, staying in a four-bedroom duplex in one of the newly developed estates in Lekki Phase 1 and wearing the best tailored suits and Italian shoes. Apart from the Toyota Prado official car which his company assigned him, Ladi had two other cars, one of which his wife used. He belonged to two of the most sought-after social clubs in Lagos and went on annual vacations with Remi, even while they dated. Although the bank funded some of these indulgences, a lot of them were paid for from his hard-earned income. When that did not measure up, he devised a convenient network from which loans could be gotten.

At the time he lost his job, Ladi's savings, in three separate accounts, amounted to a little over one million naira. He feared that this meant trouble but consoled himself with the hope that his knowledge of the banking industry would put him in a good stead for prompt re-employment with other banks. But this did not happen.

Five years after the abrupt end of his means of livelihood, he finally gave up on the prospects of ever finding another bank job. Needless to say, he had by then run out of his meagre savings and started to live from hand to mouth with his wife.

The first major expense they ran into was his rent, four months after he lost his job. Not even all the savings he had could pay for the apartment they stayed in, so the new couple moved out, far away from the Lekki neighbourhood.

They scouted for a reasonable accommodation in Ajah and Lagos mainland for about three months, before eventually finding a place that matched their taste and pocket in the Ifako area of Gbagada.

At this point, life was a far cry from how he had lived in the past few years, he now had to park his two cars outside the tiny compound where his landlord also stayed. He would drive all over town for the next several months, submitting applications, attending interviews and soliciting for help without success. Remi also attempted to return to banking, but the jobs were just not forthcoming until it was time to renew their rent again.

When the couple arrived at this juncture, the only logical thing to do was to sell off one of their two cars – a 2008 Toyota Corolla. They retained the Honda CRV, an SUV which they saw as stronger, more prestigious and capable of preserving them from the contempt of people who thought things weren't looking good for them.

But the CRV only ensured the prestige of its owners for another year. By then, their rent was due again. By this time, Ladi and Remi had tried their hands on several things. They had invested money in the coal exportation business of one of Remi's uncles, but that failed. Remi had also tried her hands on trading, getting clothes and accessories from friends who travelled abroad and selling them to ladies in banks and insurance companies. But the profit she made on these items, did not amount to much, as customers defaulted paying back.

So, to retain their apartment, off went their remaining vehicle. While Ladi continued to search for employment opportunities anywhere, his wife pursued female bankers with her clothes and accessories.

Then, Ladi began to complain about his wife. First, it was that she no longer felt accountable to him. Next, he complained that she came home late, without apology or explanations. Remi attributed this to the difficulty she had with commuting. The matter was finally laid to rest.

He later started to complain that she no longer respected him. Arguments became an everyday event in their home and Ladi blamed himself for the trouble between him and his wife. He decided to intensify his job search and find ways to keep tabs on Remi's business deals.

It was at this time that the family began to occasionally engage the services of Rasaki. Whenever Remi had business trips to make or Ladi had an important interview, Rasaki was hired to take them to their destination; an arrangement which suited the couple's need to maintain their prestige.

Ironically, when Ladi would see another ray of hope, he was without the prestige that Rasaki and his faithful Mercedes bestowed. This was about six months back.

He had been on his way to get a loaf of bread one morning, and just as he crossed the road, a 2012 Range Rover drove past him and stopped. He observed the driver reversing the vehicle and yelling out of his window.

It took Ladi only a few seconds to realise that the man sitting behind the wheel was his school mate and friend, Adams. He rushed toward the car shouting affectionately: "Adamu osha!" Adams gave his friend a firm handshake and a bear hug.

Within minutes, they were inside Ladi's apartment where they quickly caught up on old times. Playboy that he was, Adams had remained unmarried although he had two children by different women. He now lived in the United Arab Emirates (UAE) where he presided over his father's expansive real estate business.

His host told his own story and how things had been really difficult for him and Remi. Adams listened attentively and promised that he would do his best to assist this old friend of his whose happiness was important to him.

"Oh my God, I am so sorry my friend. I feel so terrible I have been far away from you," Adams said. He did not wait for his friend's response before he asked: "By the way, where is Remi, that sexy lady of yours. Is she still as hot as I remember her?"

Ladi's face contoured into a smile of pride, which soon dissolved into confusion about the rather intimate compliments his friend was giving his wife.

"I don't understand…" he started, throwing up his hand at his friend in bewilderment.

Adams smiled mischievously and squeezed his shoulder. He was about to talk when they were interrupted by a rap on the door and the entry of the lady of the house.

Remi stood transfixed for a moment, surprised at Adams's presence before throwing her wares on the floor and jumping on Adams like a child. They staggered and landed on the couch, the weight of Remi's body on Adams. Ladi stood, smiling awkwardly at his wife's reaction to his old friend.

"See who's here!" Remi said, gazing at Adams. "Look at you!" She examined him from head to toe. "Where have you been for goodness' sake?"

"Here and there, it's really good to see you guys again."

They spent another thirty minutes talking about their university days, what each of them had been up to, and what had happened to the few mutual friends they had. Adams then steered the conversation toward what could be done to alleviate their situation, especially as he was scheduled to fly out of the country that same evening.

After about an hour, he promised to try to get Ladi a job in one of his father's companies. They also decided that Remi would start a jewellery business, which Adams promised to fund with an initial five million naira. They agreed that she would make a trip to Dubai two weeks later, after Adams would have facilitated her visa, procured a flight ticket for her and gotten resident agents to assist her with shopping in Dubai.

His friends could not believe the sudden change in situation, they could not but thank God for this chance meeting that brought them back into each other's lives. While husband and wife rejoiced, Adams excused himself and returned with two bundles of ₦1000 notes. He handed them over to Ladi, whose mouth was agape in utter disbelief of how well the day was turning out.

It had been six months, but things hadn't been as smooth as Ladi had hoped. Adams's father, with whom he spoke regularly, had assured him of a good position in one of the newly licensed power generation companies he had major interests in. The only problem was that the company would not take off for a few months and so, he had been waiting.

But the situation was rosier with Remi who had been in Dubai twice in the last six months, much to her husband's discomfort. He relished those days when he was the effective breadwinner of the family and longed for them again.

His wife's first trip was largely exploratory. It was one month after the meeting with Adams. She was away for two weeks and came back with a few pieces, which were quickly bought off her. Husband and wife felt this new venture must indeed have heaven's seal.

As soon as her customers paid up, she embarked on the second trip, which had been about three weeks. This was a longer journey because her husband had been favoured with a small contract to supply medical equipment to the specialist hospital owned by Adams's father. Since it came about the time that she was making her trip to Dubai, they decided that she should work with her agents, purchase the equipment and send them down through one of the regular courier services at Dubai.

The consignment was what Ladi and Rasaki were going to receive at the Isolo office of *We Deliver Safely Logistics*. His wife had called the previous night to give him the details he needed to claim the goods, and to let him know that she would be on a flight back the next day. So, when his phone rang just as they drove into the premises of the logistics company and he saw his wife's name, he wondered what could be amiss.

It turned out to be a very short conversation in which Remi wanted to draw his attention to a letter enclosed in the carton of stethoscopes. She asked that her husband speak to her after seeing the letter and hung up with the usual, "I miss you."

It took all of thirty minutes for Ladi to clear the five boxes of equipment that his wife had couriered to him. While signing the documents presented to him by the clerk, he asked Rasaki to load the boxes into the boot with the exception of the one with the stethoscopes, which he planned to take with him in the back, so he could read his wife's love note.

As soon as he sunk into the back seat and Rasaki started the engine of the car, Ladi, with a wide smile on his face, tore open the seal of the box of stethoscopes. He found the letter he was searching for and put the box beside him. With steady hands and a wide grin lighting up his face, he tore open the note to reveal Remi's neat and familiar handwriting.

My dear Ladipupo,
I should start by thanking you for all that you have been to me in close to ten years. When you could, you did your best to make me happy and I appreciate all of it. But you will agree with me that things have not been really good with us lately. On a lot of occasions, I actually have found myself asking whether we truly loved each other from the beginning…

Ladi was not sure where this was going, he paused to wipe the balls of sweat that had started to form on his forehead with a handkerchief. He continued reading:

Let me make this easy for both of us, my darling. I regret to say that I am no longer able to stay in this marriage. It is not just that I am tired of it, but I have also found another love. Sometimes, I feel so much for you that I do not want to tell you this, but then, I also think that the earlier you know, the better. I also think that I deserve my happiness even if it will hurt you.

Since my first trip to Dubai, I have found the man that my heart is really after and I am sorry to say that I will not be coming back to you in Nigeria at the moment. By the special grace of God, I, and the man that I just found, whose baby I am now carrying, Adams…

Here, Ladi let out a loud cry: "Park this car, Rasaki. Park this car now!"

Rasaki, startled at the sudden outburst, found a good place to park the car. Ladi, tears and sweat dripping all over his face, stepped out of the car. The names of his wife and friend loud on his lips.

II

Right From the Cradle

As I stepped out of my bedroom that Tuesday morning, my eyes locked with Ochuko's. I looked away almost instantly, although, I could have sworn that she offered a conspiratorial smile and a wink. It was a most awkward moment that left me embarrassed.

Driving to work moments later, I struggled to dismiss thoughts that the girl smiled and winked at me. The mere contemplation made me feel dirty, ungodly even. She was too close, too young and too harmless to nurse the kind of thoughts I was imagining. I dismissed the idea and promised never to think of it again.

I recalled the very first day I saw Ochuko and shook my head in disgust at myself. She was a cute but shy two-year-old who clung to her mother like wet clothes on the body. I had been on my way back from work, less than forty-hours after I moved into the compound they lived, when I ran into mother and child – one dragging the other toward their flat. The woman looked back when I opened the gate and said warmly: "Good evening o," a curious look on her face.

Too tired from the tedium of packing into the compound and the day's stress, I mumbled a patently dismissive "Good evening madam," and proceeded toward my own part of the compound. But she pretended not to notice my lack of interest and continued to make conversation, even started moving toward me.

"Wait now, Oga. It's like you and your friends are our new neighbours."

I was not in the mood for small talk, but then, I thought that since this was the place, I would call home for some time, I should be friendly to the lady. I moved a step towards them. The little girl shrieked and pulled at her mother's wrapper as if she had seen a ghost.

Although I was shocked, I smiled and moved closer. Stretching my hands to her, I said: "Young lady, do I look like the angel of death. What are we screaming about?" She recoiled away from me, by which time her mother picked her up, the little girl rested on her mother's shoulders in comfort.

"Don't mind the spoilt girl, *broda*. She just likes clinging to me. It is not her fault though, I breastfed her for too long."

I wondered where this talk was going to and was thinking of a way out of the growing awkwardness when we heard a horn at the gate.

The lady instantly became unsettled. "Ah, Ochuko, that's your father. Oga, please I need to attend to my husband," she said hurriedly, straddling the child on her back and immediately scurrying toward the gate like a rat chased by a cat.

I was confused at the dramatic transformation, but it was not my business. More importantly, I was happy to finally be rid of her and walked on into my flat. Yet, I was unable to resist the temptation of watching from my window to see what would happen. The woman opened the gate to let a car in. Again, she hurried to close the gate, and then rushed to the passenger's side of the car to bring out an office bag. By then, the driver had emerged from the car and moved on toward their door. I shook my head at the queerness of it all.

Fifteen years later, that timid Ochuko had become a seventeen-year-old secondary school leaver who had become closer to my family. I stayed on in the compound even after my friends left the flat at the Adeniyi Jones area of Ikeja. The Oyides, Ochuko's family, occupied the other flat in the compound.

The father, Engineer Oyide, was a middle-level engineer with a food manufacturing company at Ikeja. His wife, apparently of only modest education, was a distributor of products from the company her husband worked for. She had a shop in the central Ikeja area, although she was at home a lot in those early days. Their two children were only four and two at the time, so she stayed home to take care of them.

The woman was more generous than her husband in a lot of ways. She talked our ears off often, but my friends and I loved her because she came to our aid even without soliciting. Mrs. Oyide stepped in to make up for almost all our inadequacies as bachelors and that included intervening in the crises with the girls who thronged our home, shopping for us occasionally and even giving us food when we were broke.

My friends and I thought her husband did not approve of her niceness to us. Not that he said or did anything to show disapproval, but he appeared too stern to have a fondness for us. He was the kind who got out of the car quickly, grumbled a greeting and never left an opportunity for small talk. Even at the monthly sanitation exercise we came together for, he barely spoke to anyone. When you greeted him, he would mutter a response, do what he had to do and move on.

That had to change when my friends moved out of the house five years into our tenancy. First, it was Tonye in preparation for his wedding. One year later, Ayo followed suit and a quantum of loneliness hit me. Mrs. Oyide was of course as friendly as ever and by now, we had lived in the same compound for about seven years during which we conceded some motherly role to her. But now alone, there were limits to how close I could remain to Mama Ochuko, I was mostly left in my own company after work, so I had to court Mr. Oyide's friendship somehow.

I found a perfect opportunity one Saturday morning when a neighbour's vehicle crashed into our fence. We were sitting in our homes when we heard a bang and ran out to see what could have happened. Engineer, as I would later start to address him, came out just about the same time as I. He had apparently just woken up and still had his oversized pyjamas on. He threw a questioning glance at me as if he expected me to have an explanation for the noise.

"What the hell is this?" he asked as we moved closer. By now, everyone in his household had joined us. He threw a glance at them and they scampered back inside like rabbits into a hole. He did not even say a word.

"I wonder sir…" I replied, still dazed by the terrorism I just witnessed.

Engineer took a look at me and smiled. I was wondering what had amused him when he cut into my thoughts.

"You are shocked at the way my people ran back into the house, right?"

Embarrassed that he could read my mind accurately, I opened my mouth to say something in denial, but he interrupted me.

"It's okay, my brother, you must be really strong with women and children, otherwise they will run riot. What were they coming to do outside?"

I could only nod, even though I disagreed with him. While I truly did not see what business the children had being out, I thought that their mother could at least be there. But then, it was his family, and I had no say.

We got to the fallen part of our fence but there was no one in the car. Engineer was just about to speak when what looked like a congregation came out of the next compound. The permanent secretary who owned the house was at the head of the people who filed out. He opened his mouth in surprise when he saw his prized vehicle hanging on the fence. When he looked back at his family members, the boy who appeared like the youngest took a few steps back, trepidation written all over his face.

"I am coming back to you later," the man threatened, just as he arrived the spot where we were standing. He told the story.

The young fifteen-year-old boy had toyed with the idea of driving for a while. Even though he had broached the subject a couple of times, his parents usually laughed it off with promises that he would learn to drive at the appropriate time.

"Children of nowadays run far ahead of their time," the perm sec told us, as he pleaded for understanding. "I am grateful to God that no one got injured, but we will deal with this immediately," he concluded and shook hands with us.

Engineer, seeing that the perm sec was about to return to his house, held on to his hand.

"I hope sir, that this young man will get some discipline though. This behaviour is so terribly out of line and should not be treated with levity because..."

"Thank you for your advice. I assure you I know what to do. I apologise again for the trouble we have caused," The perm sec replied, snatched his hand from Engineer's grip and walked into his house without even looking back.

Engineer and I talked for most of the remaining part of that day. While supervising the work on our fence, he asked so many questions that when I ruminated over our conversation on retiring to my apartment later that evening, I felt like a naked man. Yet, I was happy that we talked, especially as he, from that day, became more friendly.

He started by asking what I did for a living. We talked about my friends. I told him they moved out because they got married – a curious information to share years after they had left. He asked about my parents, where I came from and when I planned to get married like my friends.

"I plan to get married in the coming year, sir," I replied with enthusiasm.

"Oh lovely," he responded with a bland face that suggested anything but lovely.

He read my confusion and laughed hysterically – that confused me even more. What exactly was the problem? Did he know anything about Joy, the girl I planned to marry or what was this about?

"You know, sometimes, I wonder if marriage is worth all the fuss, we make about it ..." he finally offered. "I wasn't going to get married at all. I just couldn't stand the trouble of women, which I saw in my mother. Ironically, it was also because of her that I got married. She was going to kill me with talk about carrying on the family name and all that, so I decided to do it. And that is what we have, he said pointing towards his flat."

I was stunned. Words eluded me and then I realised he wasn't finished.

"Don't bother to say anything, my brother. You will soon realise what I am saying, but it's fine. Even, I have recently concluded that women have their usefulness. At least, I have two adorable children and there is someone to take care of them and keep the home. For me that is enough, so I encourage you to do it. I can only wish you the best." He patted me on the back with a finality that gave me no opportunity to respond.

I had a completely different opinion and would have loved to share it with him, but he already showed that was the end of the discussion and that he wasn't interested in whatever I had to say. I let it slide but we became closer after that.

He allowed me some proximity to his family, I could now sit down with him in his living room to discuss politics, religion and what-have you. His wife was more comfortable to deal with me, and his children came around to mine now and then, sometimes shouting my name right from their parents' door. This was more so with Ochuko who I began to call "small wife," since the day I reminded her mother of the story of our first meeting.

This went on even after I got married. The children continued to see my home as an extension of theirs, and Joy, my wife, treated them as family. And when I called the young girl "small wife," we all just laughed at what we knew was just a joke. Things went on very well until my wife and I bought over the house we lived in and the Oyides suddenly became our tenants.

Just before we finalised the agreement for the takeover of the house, we felt it was important to let the family know our plans and the decision to write off their rent for the next two years. Engineer lost his job when the company he worked for ran into some trouble with the banks. We felt our offer would alleviate the family's trouble while he worked towards getting another job. We decided to visit early one Saturday morning.

"Who is there?" the lady of the house said in answer to our knock.

"Your landlords," I whispered mischievously into Joy's ears. She smiled and gave me a feeble nudge in my side. We both giggled excitedly. "Daniel and Joy. Mama Ejiro, good morning."

"Oh, good morning Mr. Daniel. Please give me one minute," she responded and let us in.

A moment later, Engineer joined us in the living room. After commiserating with him over the loss of his job, I cleared my throat to speak. A tinge of nervousness came over me, but I told myself that there really wasn't anything to worry about.

"Engineer, we came to inform you that we have been talking to the landlord about buying this house," I started and then paused, waiting to see the effect of my words on my listeners. If the Oyides were surprised, they did nothing to show it, and this confirmed our suspicion that information might have filtered to them through the landlord, his lawyer or one of the other people who knew about the deal.

There was a minute of silence in which no one said a word, not even a congratulatory note from the Oyides. I chose to continue.

"So, Engineer, the landlord told us that your rent will be due soon." Again, I paused for effect and noticed the muscles on his face tighten, he scratched his head, sat up on his seat and then momentarily relaxed again. I felt glad that this statement made them realise who was in charge. It was a moment of sadistic pleasure, which immediately assuaged my disappointment in their failure to congratulate us earlier.

I continued: "Joy and I understand the current situation of things and have decided to let you stay in your apartment rent free for the next two years."

Engineer's face brightened up with a broad smile. He made like he was going to jump up out of his seat but thought better of it, and just as suddenly as the smile appeared before, it disappeared.

My wife and I looked at each other, shocked at how much our new tenant was trying to make things difficult.

It didn't look like anything we said here would impress this family, still I was glad we broke the news to them. The next few minutes were filled with a discomforting silence, so I thought we should leave.

"It's alright, we should…" I started to talk about the need for us to return to our flat when Mama Ejiro cut in.

"Oh, we thank you people for your kindness, we are really grateful for what you have done. God bless you." She clasped her hands together.

Suddenly, Engineer's smile returned and brightened up the mood in the room. He thanked us for the kind offer and promised that he would do everything to cooperate with us in whatever we chose to do with our new house.

"I am very grateful for your kindness. I am sure God sent you to assist us and the same God, will bless you," he said in what seemed to be his final word and a signal for us to return to our flat. He was on his feet before ending the sentence, extending his hands towards me.

We walked out like rain-beaten chickens but still thought we did the right thing and had no reason to worry over the Oyides.

"It is your mission to the market you consider, not the noise of the market, Daniel. We were concerned about our relationship with this family and how to alleviate their misfortune. We have offered help; it doesn't matter how they received it. We have done our own part and the heavens see our hearts," my wife said, when I kept grumbling over Engineer's continued aloofness. "I am sure they will soon come around, so don't worry about it so much, my darling." She drew me close and planted a kiss on my lips.

True to her words, things got better between our families. Although Engineer behaved like someone whose brain was controlled by a remote with faulty batteries, sometimes pleasant and other times, difficult. His family were almost always kind and respectful. And this time around, it seemed like he let them be, possibly a fallout of his economic realities.

Engineer hadn't been able to secure another job, so he relied on occasional contracts from his old classmates and friends. This brought a lot of pressure on the family, part of which diminished his self-esteem. Mama Ejiro came to us whenever she needed help, and her children felt comfortable bringing their challenges to my wife, who always had a listening ear. Ochuko reached out to me through text messages once in a while. Those messages would usually start with "uncle boo", and at other times, "how is my favourite uncle doing at work today." We would then chat for a few minutes about school, family and work. In one of those discussions, she had told me she wanted to study Mass Communication and could do with some mentoring from me. I assured her I would always be available.

At this time, Ejiro had one year to complete his university education. Ochuko had sat for and passed her university matriculation exam and was only awaiting the result of her secondary school certificate before pursuing university admission. It was five years into my marriage and God had blessed us with a set of twins just at the time that we planned. After three months of maternity leave, my wife had to return to her job at the bank. Since Ochuko was home awaiting her results, Joy arranged with Mama Ejiro for her to babysit for us. It was a perfect arrangement for everyone. Joy could return to work while Ochuko took care of the children and earned some money in preparation for the university.

I did my best to avoid the trouble that another look at Ochuko portended, but things did not work my way. After a few more days, I was convinced that her look was not just in my imagination. Ochuko spoke more boldly to me and even once came into my room without knocking, although she swore she did. Fortunately, I was dressed and about to step out. I sensed danger; I had started imagining all sort of things with this young girl, and I knew it was not good at all. That evening, I proposed that Joy and I reconsider the babysitting arrangement, but she would not hear of it.

"Oh, please, Daniel. I have a lot of peace knowing that the twins are with Ochuko. Where do we start looking for a stranger who will not come into our home and harm the children?" Joy thundered, bewildered at my request.

"We won't pick just anyone on the streets, darling. We will go through one of these agencies…"

"No, please. Agency or no agency, anyone we bring here will be a stranger. I cannot be at work and still worry about the safety of my children. This girl is literally family and your fear about her father starting any trouble is unfounded," Joy threw back. "Where is this coming from *sef*?" she continued. I tried to explain but she went on. "Seriously, just out of nowhere you think Engineer might start trouble because his daughter works for us and we pay her? Why didn't you say this at the beginning?"

At that point, I knew we were beginning to tread on slippery turf. I backtracked, hoping to bring up the issue another time.

"Alright, alright, no need to bring down the roof, you win. Let her stay." I stormed out of our bedroom just to put an end to the contention.

For the next three weeks, things went on smoothly even though there were moments when my resolve was tested. Ochuko gave me no further reasons to be wary of her. She was almost always dressed in clothes that accentuated her physical endowments which got to me every single time, but I managed to keep it together. In spite of myself, I got closer to her. We talked and laughed about a variety of things, including the welfare of the twins and her resolve to be a famous television presenter. I even once asked if she had a boyfriend, but she laughed it off without answering. In retrospect, I was thankful that she provided no response because I most likely would have pursued the issue.

Ochuko came in at 6 a.m., so my wife could properly hand over to her before leaving for work thirty minutes later. Since I didn't leave for work until between 9 and 10 a.m. every day, I would usually go back to bed for another half hour, watch a breakfast show on television during which Ochuko and I would usually gist. The twins had a routine of sleeping until about 10 am, so we talked without interruption until I had to take a bath at about 8:45 a.m. and head for work thereafter.

Then, what I feared came upon me one otherwise quiet morning. I had returned home about ten minutes after I left to pick up a document I needed for a meeting. Knowing that Ochuko would be in the twins' room watching over them, I let myself into the house and quietly made into our room. As I opened the door, there was Ochuko, in her underwear, checking out herself in the bathroom mirror. The sight overwhelmed me. Shocked to see me back so soon, she opened her mouth to speak, but I was already on her, my lips totally swallowing hers.

Thinking about it now, I marvel at the speed at which I rushed at her. I cannot remember if she put up any resistance, but if she did, it must have been too feeble for me to notice. Whatever came over me took total control, and I left the world and all its worries behind me. From feasting on her lips, it happened. I finally made true the thoughts I had had since that Tuesday morning, but after the pleasure of that moment, a cloud of shame enveloped me. I swore that it would never happen again and apologised to Ochuko for taking advantage of her.

But then, like the dog that delights in returning to its vomit, it kept happening for a few more weeks. It was very convenient. I worked for myself and could choose to stay home all day if I liked. The twins were too unaware to be any source of worry, and Engineer, who stayed most of the day in his room was too unconcerned about what his daughter or anyone was doing. Ochuko, young as she was, was a perfect collaborator. Unassuming and dutiful in every ramification, never giving my wife cause for suspicion.

But the seed we sowed in private soon sprouted; Ochuko told me she had missed her period. When I got the WhatsApp message, I thought it was a joke because we had had one of our scintillating sessions earlier and she hadn't betrayed any emotions. I had packed my bag, ready to go home, when her message came in.

Uncle Daniel, we need to talk. It was an unusual message. First, I had not been *Uncle Daniel* to her in a long time, and second, *we need to talk* was an odd tone. But even that did not prepare me for the impending shock.

What is it my darling? I wrote back, attaching an indulgent blushing emoji.

I am worried, Uncle. My period is really late, I hope…

Huh? You hope what? I suddenly started feeling a headache.

I had a barrage of questions for her over the next few minutes and then I went on a voyage of recollection. How could pregnancy have resulted when we always had protection? Then I remembered the first time that we didn't plan for, and the day Ochuko promised to dispose the condom for me. Could she have done anything funny? But what could she have done, I wondered? Cautioning myself to stop the needless self-questioning, I realised that we were not even sure she was pregnant.

I concluded that she needed a home test and decided to get a test kit for her on my way home. We agreed that I would find a way to slip it into her bag in the likely event that my wife got home ahead of me. I grabbed my car keys, drove to the pharmacy three streets away, and headed home.

Joy was home as I anticipated, but at the time I arrived, she was in the twins' room, taking over from Ochuko who had smartly left her clutch bag on the dining table. I slipped the test kit into it.

Of course, I couldn't sleep that entire night. I tossed and turned in bed like a restless lion in a cage. It was worse because all attempts to reach Ochuko remained futile, my messages did not deliver and when I snuck into the bathroom to call her, her phone was switched off. Anxiety almost killed me. Fortunately, Joy slept like a well-fed baby, so she had no idea what I was going through.

In the morning, there was a discomforting silence from our tenants' flat. That didn't make things easier. By 6.30 a.m. when Joy was leaving the house, we saw no sign of Ochuko and that frightened the life out of me. Joy wanted to go knock on their door, but I dissuaded her.

"I will be home until she comes, so you just go right ahead. Fortunately, they are still asleep," I said about the twins, guiding her into her car.

I was barely back in the house when I heard a banging on the door. With it came Engineer's loud voice shattering the peace the peace of the morning:

"Daniel! You dog! Open this door before I break it down!" He continued to bang the door.

I immediately got the gist. He already knew the truth and was here to cause trouble. Whatever it was, I was grateful that Joy had left the house before he turned up. The news would have ruined her day. I moved speedily to the door. I needed to bring him in before he drew the attention of the neighbourhood.

"Good morning, Engineer, please come in…"

"Pocket your good morning, Mr. Cradle Snatcher. So, you see no other person to seduce but my underaged daughter? You are in trouble that your generations unborn will be unable to handle."

I could not pretend that I didn't know what he was talking about, but I needed him to lower his voice.

"Please come in, Engineer, and let us talk, it is very early…"

"You didn't know it was early when you were sampling my daughter, you shameless man. I made a mistake; I should have come here before your wife left!"

Now, he had stepped into the house and at that point, it dawned on me that coming to see me after Joy had left for work was deliberate. I wondered why he was being so considerate, but I was grateful.

"So, you raped my daughter."

"I did not…"

"You better shut up, you shameless dog! Because you have a wife that feeds you, you won't let a small girl rest. You exploited the misfortune in my family and put my daughter in the family way," he continued ranting. I opened my mouth to explain but he waved me to a stop with his hand.

"Now, listen, I want to give you the opportunity to redeem yourself before telling your wife."

"Thank you, sir, I…"

"Shut up and listen. You raped my underaged daughter and I am going to ensure that you go to jail unless you do what I want."

"I will do anything sir…"

"Not sure you have much of a choice. That flat that I live in, you are going to sign it over to me like I bought it from you. You are also going to pay me the sum of five million naira within the next one week."

I opened my mouth but found no words after he reeled out his conditions.

"If you like open your mouth and let flies enter it," he continued. "If you do not meet these conditions within the week, I am going to start by telling your wife and reporting this matter to the police."

He walked away with a long hiss.

I looked at him, tears rolling down my cheeks. This was the greatest dilemma of my entire life, one which I had to resolve in one week if I did not want to go to jail and lose my family to boot. I wondered where I would start from.

It had been o

more than j

of the mass

notes. So, I

with this w

dance to blowjob and threesome all in one night.

All done, yours truly was still half high and spent as I staggered home after alighting from the Bolt cab that drove me from the club. Taxis were a rare luxury in the life that I lived. They came on few occasions when I met men with heavy pockets and a sense of sexual adventure like this night.

As I shut the door, one of those ubiquitous Lagos commercial buses known as *danfo* pulled up at the bus stop just ahead of me. Even though it was still a bit dark, I saw a young lady jump out of the bus. She took two or three quick leaps immediately she landed on the ground. That drew my attention. *How can a lady, who most certainly didn't have a good night's sleep be so athletic at this time of the morning?*

She looked back, increased her pace and looked back again. On impulse, I turned back to see if there was [redacted] from, but beyond the few [redacted] was no visible sign of danger. I [redacted] looking back again after which [redacted]. This time, I noticed she had a bag [redacted]. I wondered what the problem was [redacted] find out. Just then, she turned onto the dirt [redacted] to the shanties that I call home, looked back [redacted] then leapt forward.

“Excuse me,” I said, increasing my pace to catch up [redacted] her. Her reaction showed that I had frightened her more. She looked back and in fact, took to her heels this time. I was dumbfounded.

“No, I didn’t mean to startle you. I’m sorry, please stop!” I shouted, instantly drawing back. I imagined there was no need to run after her since nothing was at stake for me. In any case, I was too exhausted from fulfilling the fantasies of my last client. When I noticed she did not stop, I decided to let her be, after all, I was safe.

And then she stopped. Like a lost dog that suddenly heard the whistle of its owner, she walked back towards me. I paused for a moment. Was this lady mentally stable? Could she be carrying a weapon or was she just high? These thoughts ran through my mind in quick succession in the time it took for her to get very close to me. I took a step or two backwards and then she spoke.

“Sorry, I embarrassed you. I just wanted to be safe,” she said in a childlike pitch that would melt a heart of stone.

"Oh dear, it's alright. But what were you afraid of?" I walked, too tired to stand for long on the road. "Which way are you headed by the way?" I added as an afterthought.

"There," she said, pointing to what we would both later jokingly refer to as our block of flats.

"Are you kidding? I stay there as well," I said, totally shocked at the revelation and the fact that I hadn't run into her before.

Her eyes widened with excitement and then narrowed. I couldn't but wonder what that was about, but I chose not to probe.

"There" was a makeshift community of shanties arbitrarily created by unemployed, untrained youths of the Sarako area of Lekki. They called our section of the growing community, Olokoode and it was made of two lines of cubicles housing about fifty people who all shared two bathrooms and toilets. It didn't matter whether you were male or female. When nature called, you went into any of these rooms. God help you if you ran into a queue of residents also waiting to answer the call of nature.

I recall an incident when while about ten people were waiting to use the toilet, what started like mere loud, but inoffensive farts from one of the men suddenly produced the most messy and smelly shit I have witnessed in my twenty-five years. Faeces poured on him uncontrollably, like water from a faulty tap, and in an instant, everyone standing in line fled like some evil spirit was after them.

In spite of the terrible facilities, we were happy there was somewhere to lay our heads after the hustle of every day. It was also a secure place. These boys were the lords of the area and no criminal, who was not ready to join his ancestors, would venture into Olokoode or any of the other settlements around the peninsula. Even security agents and local government officials who harassed and added to the misery of ordinary citizens overlooked our excesses. They learned this after one of them was castrated for attempting to rape a female resident. We learnt that such incidents had happened on one or two occasions in the past, so the boys chose to make an example of this he-goat in uniform.

Yet, we paid for all of this in one way or the other – the boys made us pay. They increased the rent on a whim. You could pay one thousand-naira one day and be requested to pay three thousand the next. And if you failed to pay, you got a twenty-four-hour notice to pay or leave. Who could you report to? This was the kind of situation in which we lived.

"How long have you been here?" I asked. I sensed a hesitation, so to put her at ease, I gave her unsolicited information about myself. "I have been here for three years and I hope to leave at the end of this year when I finish school."

A sudden glow crept out of her hitherto subdued face "Oh, you are in school? Which one? How did you get here?"

I laughed at her sudden enthusiasm, wondering which of these questions I should answer first. I pointed in the direction of our abode to indicate that we should walk along.

"I don't even know your name," I said, giving her my best smile. "Mine is Benita and I am pleased to meet someone I can talk to in this dungeon."

She gave me a disarming smile that revealed perfect dentition, accentuated by a prominent gap in her teeth, it was truly angelic. I wanted to know her more.

"My name is Halima," she said, as we moved towards the shanty.

We agreed that both of us were too tired to go into any long discussion at that moment. So, I followed Halima to her room, which was just one lane behind mine. After exchanging phone numbers, we agreed to meet up the next day.

I attended the first service in the neighbourhood church where I worshipped and returned home by 9 a.m. Halima did not return until about 3 p.m., but I wasn't surprised. She had told me that she would be working on Sunday and our rendezvous was in the evening. We planned to talk and walk to Eleko Beach, just a short distance from our home.

My new friend could not wait for us to settle down at the beach before she fired the first question. I marvelled at how conversational she had become since our first meeting.

"So, Benita, how did you know that god-forsaken house?" she asked, laughing heartily like she had just said something that won both of us some treasure.

I smiled.

"So, I am a student at the University of Lagos," I started, but was interrupted by Halima's sudden screech after which she covered her mouth with both hands. I could only smile.

"Wait, wait, wait, you mean you are a university student?" Halima asked excitedly.

I nodded in assent.

"Wow!"

I marvelled at the way she responded to the news that I was in the university, even though I could relate. This was how I used to look at uni people before I became one. Although, I was in my final year and within months of completing my education, I could still remember how I used to envy university students.

I told her how I got introduced to the place we lived through a girl who had been roommates with another girl with whom I squatted in my first year. My "landlady", as we called those who let us share bed spaces with them, was from my village and treated me with so much kindness upon my arrival at the University of Lagos.

I completed my secondary education and passed the UME with the sheer determination to fulfil my father's life-long wish of having his only child earn a degree. So, even though he passed on just before I left secondary school, my mother and I were determined to honour his memory and make him happy in the afterlife by doing everything to ensure I attended the university.

My father's death happened like a dream; one we hoped to wake up from. He was attacked by a group of unknown bandits on his way from the farm. Found in a pool of his blood by villagers, they quickly mobilised a motorcycle to take him to the closest hospital in a village thirty minutes away from ours. We were told that he was pronounced dead on arrival, he had lost too much blood. When my results were released and they were excellent as we all anticipated, my mother and I vowed to fulfil father's wish.

Upon gaining admission into the University of Lagos, there were concerns about how I would cope in Lagos. Then, we discovered that Rhoda, one of the girls from the village, had been on the campus for three years and might be able to help me find my way through. My mother reached out to her family and contact was made with her. She accepted that I could stay in her room, but she was in her final year and wouldn't be able to accommodate me for more than one year.

"I was complaining about how I would cope after Rhoda's graduation when one of her roommates told me about this place. A girl in her class lived here and had told them it was affordable. She linked me up with the classmate who just transferred her room to me when she graduated.

What about you? Tell me your story," I concluded, looking straight into Halima's eyes.

She was staring into space as though she was in a trance. The otherwise light atmosphere became charged and by the time she seemed to have gathered herself together, tears had welled up in her eyes. That made me uncomfortable. I tried to draw her close and hug her, but she pulled back and raised her right hand to stop me.

"I came to Lagos from Kogi State some months back," she finally said.

"Oh really…?"

"And I came alone."

By now, tears were already dripping down her face. I felt sorry for her. I made another attempt to draw her to me, but she raised her hand to indicate that it was fine.

"I actually want to talk about this. I'll be fine," she said, forcing a smile.

For the next couple of minutes, I listened to her with rapt attention.

What drove Halima out of her village near Okene was an accident. It all began one day, shortly after she got registered for her school certificate examination. She had snuck out of school for what she considered to be a noble mission.

One of her classmates was unable to register for the examinations because her parents were indigent. She was the smartest girl in the class, and her friends, of which Halima was one, thought it would be a great shame if she couldn't write the exams. So, they came together and agreed to raise funds.

"The plan was to talk with our parents, but I didn't want to tell my father because he had just paid for me and my stepbrother's registration. I knew another way though. Two years ago, I discovered that he kept money in a bag under his bed and since then, I would go there and help myself to it. I decided I would get back home early and steal my contribution from my dad," she said, wiping tears off her face with a brownish handkerchief from her blue denim pants.

Knowing that her father and stepmother were not going to return from work until 4 p.m. and 2 p.m. respectively, she stole out of school just as the last lesson of the day was about to start. The walk to the house was only ten minutes and that gave her a clear twenty minutes before anyone could get back. She unlocked the door of their three-bedroom flat and dashed straight into her father and stepmother's bedroom. Halima was the only child of her mother, who ran away with another man when her daughter was just three. The stepmother was the only mother she knew. She treated Halima well and gave her no reason to feel uncared for, even though she had three children of her own, one of which was in the same class as Halima.

"Well, I got into the room and pulled out my dad's money bag from under the bed. I was about to count out the five thousand naira I wanted to take when my stepbrother burst into the room. He asked me what I was doing. I was shocked, I wished the ground would open up and swallow me, but there he was, growling at me while I wondered how he himself got there. He must have also left school to see what I was up to.

He started ranting about how I was the one who always took Dad's money while allowing everyone else to take the blame. There was nothing I said that made sense. He charged at me to take the bag, but I pushed him. He fell back and landed on his head. Suddenly, he was stiff. I shouted his name, but he didn't respond. I shook his body but there was no response, it was then that I noticed a flow of blood under his head. I wanted to die! The only thought on my mind was I had killed him. I couldn't wait for anyone to meet me at home, and I had barely fifteen minutes. I took off my uniform and left the house without knowing where I was going. I walked toward the garage. I didn't know where to go but I knew it had to be very far away from home. There were very few vehicles at that time of the day. I found one going to Lagos and decided that was my destination. I just could not wait to face the consequences of his likely death."

At this point, she broke down in tears. I couldn't stop myself from moving close and hugging her, and this time, she did not resist. She fell into my arms like a baby and wept. I didn't try to stop her, I waited until she was calm and then asked if she had made any attempt to find out what may have happened to her brother. She answered in the negative and then continued to tell me how she got into the shanty.

"Fortunately, I met no one I knew. They told me the bus was heading for Lekki, but it made no difference. By the time we arrived in Lagos, it was well past midnight. I had never been as frightened as I was that night. I was scared about what I would do, where I would sleep and if I would not become a victim of my stupidity. But something led me to speak with the driver of the bus while people were still getting off. I told him I needed somewhere to pass the night, he looked at me like I was not the same person he travelled the past ten hours with.

'Why you come Lagos when you no get where to stay?' he fired at me with irritation.

'Please, Oga, do you know anywhere I can stay?' I replied.

'Stay here, make I ask the garage boys.'

"I was so afraid that I started to cry and blame myself for embarking on this foolish journey. I thought I should at least have raised an alarm for help to see if my brother had survived, and if not, I wondered what the worst could have been. I started to regret leaving home. He returned in the company of one rough-looking guy. Noticing how frightened I was, he tried to put my mind at rest."

'Why you dey shake like fish? No worry, you dey safe, this guy na my person,' he said, pointing at the rough guy with all confidence.

He asked me if I had up to a thousand naira, I still had about two thousand naira left. He told me he wanted to finish his drink and then he would take me to a better place. That *better place* turned out to be this shanty, and that's how I got here five months ago!"

I felt bad for her, but then, life had to go on. Over the next two months, Halima and I got so close we spoke about every and anything that occurred to us. During our discussions, I revealed to her that I danced in a night club and satisfied the appetites of men for a fee whenever the opportunity arose.

I told her this way of life started in my second year when my father's only brother stopped supporting my mother and I because she had refused his sexual advances. Where I come from, it is the right of male siblings of a dead man to seek the hand of his widow in marriage. However, unlike in the past, civilisation allows the woman to reject this proposal. My mother chose to remain free from her brother-in-law turned suitor and Uncle Thompson, a prosperous family man in the village, also decided to stop supporting us.

He refused to do anything for me, the "daughter of that stubborn woman" and I, determined to complete my university education, took my destiny in my hands. I described my joy in completing my education that year and that, although I couldn't vouch that it would end my career as an alley cat, it sure was the window into the possibilities of the future.

We did not judge one another. I tried to encourage Halima to believe that whatever may have happened to her brother was not really her fault. It was nothing more than an accident. In any case, her brother was probably still alive and most importantly, what she chose to do with her new life could make up for mistakes of the past, whatever they might be.

She told me she worked as one of the admin hands at one Shepherd of the Flock Church in Ikoyi. This, she said, was why she stayed late in church on Sundays and had to be at all-night prayer meetings, like the one she was coming from on the morning we met. This information gladdened my heart. It reassured me that my new friend was on a right path.

I loved that Halima was interested in going back to school. She operated a savings account with a leading bank and was ready to sit for the school certificate exam and thereafter write JAMB, with hopes of getting into the University of Lagos to study Psychology, a discipline for which, to my surprise, she had so much passion. She was also popular. She had a friendly and generous spirit which made everyone around her comfortable and happy. Halima could give her last kobo to anyone with a pressing need, and that really made me fall in love with her and loathe the idea that we would soon be separated because I was going away for my national youth service.

By the sixth month of our meeting, I was done with school. The graduation clearance process was tedious, so Halima and I saw very little of each other. Two days before I was scheduled to leave for Kano State where I had been posted to serve, we were talking about how life was going to be for her in my absence when her phone rang. It was not unusual for any of us to get a phone call but her reaction this afternoon told me something was off.

"Hello... yes, why are you calling me?" I heard her say.

Stunned, I gestured at her.

She waved back at me to indicate that everything was alright, but her next response got me more concerned.

"But I said you shouldn't call me now," she said, getting up on her feet and making for the door.

When she did not return after some minutes, I decided to find out what was happening.

"Please don't call me again," I heard her say as I opened the door before she ended the call.

Her face had suddenly become tired and burdened like she was carrying the trouble of every single one of Nigeria's over 200 million citizens. I asked who that was as we walked back into the room.

"It's one idiot like that, abeg no worry." She said with finality, even though her face told me a different thing. We stepped back into the room and hardly took our seats when her phone rang again.

"See, I have told you not to call me again," she was saying when we heard a loud bang on the door.

I ran to the door to see who was there. What I found surprised and frightened me. Four men, one of who looked badly beaten, half-dressed and in handcuffs, were at the door. There was another man who, clean-shaven and in a pair of denim pants and a shirt, looked more respectable than the other two who were in police uniform.

The man in handcuffs was struggling to identify Halima when the guy in denim hushed him with a wave of a hand.

"I'm Ignatius James from the Crime Investigations Department. We have a search and arrest warrant for Miss Halima Shuabi. Which of you goes by that name? I opened my mouth to speak but Halima had stepped forward.

"I am the one." She stretched out her hands in surrender to be handcuffed even though no one had asked her to. Every other thing the man said was lost in a sea of confusion for me. I couldn't make any sense of the whole incident as they led Halima to her room. I rushed after them and we were there for another sixty minutes. I was shouting and crying that nothing should happen to this girl who had become like a sister to me. Halima looked stoic and taciturn with the grit of a man who has killed hundreds of souls in war. She made me feel weak, even stupid at the drama of my worry for her. At some point, the police officer instructed that they throw me out of the room and that was the only time Halima spoke, she insisted that I stay.

After about sixty minutes of a fruitless search, they asked Halima to follow them to their station at Ikate, about two kilometres from where we resided. I decided to follow them. The man in denim had no objection, except that I couldn't follow them in the small vehicle they had come in.

I stood transfixed on the spot as they sped off, pondering it all for a while. Could it be that her brother died, and they had finally traced her? Then I remembered the call she had received and perished the thought that this had to do with her brother. This was about something else, and it was something Halima had not told me about. I concluded that something was amiss. Halima was not the kind of girl to get herself enmeshed in crime.

"I am sure this is just a misunderstanding which will be resolved," I said to myself, walking back into the house.

When I got to the police station one hour later, I was told that Halima had been moved to Panti and that infuriated me. I didn't bargain for the cost of a taxi to the mainland and the demonic traffic that I envisaged at that time of the day. I took the trip regardless and got to the dreaded Panti Zonal Crime unit about two hours after I left Lekki.

At the counter, it took an annoying twenty minutes for any of the five police officers standing at the counter to speak to me. The small reception of the police station was like a marketplace with people milling about trying to gain the attention of the policemen who had more than their fair share of people to attend to. By the time a female officer looked my way, I was exhausted and sweating like a bottle of cold water. There were just two rusted and tired ceiling fans in the crowded room, and they made more noise than provide relief from the burning heat of the afternoon.

"Na that thief girl wey we carry go cell 7," one of her colleagues yelled in response to her enquiry about my request.

"Oh, na that one?" the lady said, walked away for about two minutes and came back to tell me that my friend was already in a cell and that the Investigating Police Officer for the complaint against her was going to speak to me. I was ushered into the small cubicle that served as the IPO's office about ten minutes later.

Sitting behind a small desk was a fine, well-spoken officer, like one of those you see in American films. His office, though small, looked nothing like the oven I had just come from. A small air conditioner hung on the wall opposite his desk, and he had an HP laptop in front of him. A family photograph with him in a lawyer's robe hung behind him. The small office smelt like a plantation of roses. He offered me the seat across his table. After I sat, he asked questions about me and what I did for a living. I told him I just graduated from UNILAG and was due to travel out of Lagos in two days for my national youth service.

"Your friend is in deep trouble and I don't know what you can do to save her." It sounded more like a threat than a piece of information.

"Please, sir, what did she do?" I asked.

"I am going to let you speak with her so she can talk to you herself."

He got up from his seat, walked towards the door and asked me to follow him. He led the way back to the front office, where he instructed that they bring her out of her cell to speak with me.

The Halima I saw was a shadow of herself. Her natural radiance had given way to a shabby appearance. She looked ten years older than her real age, all within just a few hours. My emotions gave way when I saw her, tears poured down my eyes like torrents of rain. Halima ran into my arms wailing and for the next couple of minutes we cried our eyes out like we were a tag team in a weeping competition. She then told me she had been severely tortured and expressed the fear that her life was not safe. I told her I would take it up with the IPO, but I couldn't wait to understand it all.

"So, what are they saying you did…?" I began.

Halima shared the most unbelievable revelations I ever heard.

Apparently, she had been stealing from churches since she came to Lagos. She went from church to church on Sundays, Wednesdays and Fridays when they held vigils, and waited for moments when members were at their most vulnerable to take their belongings. On certain Sundays, my friend confessed that she operated in as many as three different churches!

"I know the services attended by the big people in these churches. I wait for the moment they are most relaxed and steal their valuables," she confessed, barely looking up at my confused and angry face.

At this point, one of the policemen I met at the counter announced that time was up and took her back into her cell before I could protest. I returned to the IPO who gave me details of Halima's last job.

She had joined worshippers for Sunday service at the Catholic Church of Ascension, Victoria Island, three weeks back. And at some point, when the congregation was praying, Halima slid into a seat beside an obviously rich lady and took off with her Hermes handbag. She went into the bathroom, took the matching clutch purse, which she found in the handbag, all the money in the bag, as well as the lady's iPhone 11 Max. She thereafter dropped the bag in the bathroom, apparently to avoid being noticed.

"And she got away! Your friend is quite good at this thing. We are still questioning the security boys at the church on how she slipped away, but she is good," the IPO explained.

Unfortunately, the clutch bag Halima went away with had the keys to the SUV the woman drove to church in and that left the lady stranded. She reported the matter to the police, who started to track her phone. And that was where Halima dropped the ball: she called the receiver of all her stolen items with the phone and after three weeks, the police traced the call to this man who eventually led them to Halima, his regular supplier.

"The woman is not so angry about the phone or money. That she was stranded and had to join the vehicle of another church member to get home is the most painful part for her. She insists that we must take the matter to court and is determined to send this girl to jail. And there truly isn't anything we can do about it. Her car is still in the church premises. We need your friend to tell us what happened to the key. Did she tell you anything about that?"

"No, our discussion was cut short by one officer. He said time was up."

"Oh, who did that? I told them to let you have enough time with her."

He stood up from his seat, opened the door to the office and shouted. "Cynthia!" Within seconds, the lady at the counter appeared and took instructions that they should allow me to speak to Halima for as long as we wanted to. And so, she was brought out a second time.

Halima met me with tears once again. She apologised for all the deceit and how much I had been through within a few hours. Even though I was upset, I dismissed her theatrics with a wave of my hand.

"Hush. Please, where is the car key?"

She burst into another loud bout of cries; I couldn't fathom what it was about. Noticing the confused look on my face, she offered:

"I threw it away, Benny. I don't know what got into me, but I threw the key away before I sold the bag," she said, crying even harder so that I was moved to tears.

We discussed for a few more minutes before they asked her to return to her cell. I asked her a lot of questions even though I knew she would be unable to provide immediate answers. I reminded her that I had to report to the NYSC orientation camp the next day but that I would talk to the IPO and do my best to find the woman whose item she had stolen and see if we could find a way out. As disappointed and upset as I was, I remembered that we were two girls who seemed to have no one but each other, so I decided to spend the whole of the next day trying to find a solution. I could travel to Kano the day after and still be in time for the swearing in.

That day went by so fast it broke my heart. Regardless of efforts by the policemen, who had now told the woman that the car key could not be found, I was unable to see her. She told the IPO that she was not going to have any discussions with "the thief or any member of her miserable family." All she wanted was that the girl should have her day in court. I burst into tears when I was told.

"Tears will do nothing for you at this time. You need to think about getting a lawyer for her."

"Ah!" I started to cry again. "How do I go about that? We don't even have money."

"In that case, the state will assign a lawyer to her from the Legal Aid Council. You do not have to worry about it," said the IPO, who in spite of his firmness, had shown so much understanding for Halima's situation. He promised to do his best for Halima since I had to travel the following day, and that I had nothing to worry about.

Before I left the police station at about 7 p.m., I had five minutes to speak with Halima. I told her about the lawyer. She said she had money in her account with which we could hire a lawyer, but I dismissed the idea as unnecessary since the state could provide a lawyer for free. In any case, I would not be around to see if I could hire the lawyer.

I assured her that the IPO had promised to make it easy for us to speak when I got to the camp and that I would call as often as I could in the course of my journey the next day. I assured her that all would be well and that she should keep the faith. Then, I left.

The journey to Kano was nothing like I thought. I got to the motor park at Obalende at 5.30 a.m. and met a swarm of other prospective corps members travelling to different parts of the country. It was a real struggle. Our bus finally took off at around 7 a.m. but we travelled for about sixteen hours. It remains the most strenuous event of my life.

Although my mind was on Halima throughout the journey, I could only communicate with the IPO who told me that a lawyer had been appointed for Halima and that she was going to be arraigned in court the next morning. He was asking one of his subordinates to get her from the cell when the call disconnected. I tried to call back several times without luck before my phone eventually went off.

We arrived at the orientation camp, Karaye, Kano, at about 11 p.m. I was dead tired, yet it was not anyway near the end of the day for us. We immediately started a registration exercise that lasted until after 1 a.m., before we went to get some sleep, only to be woken up at 5 a.m.

I was distraught at my inability to call Lagos. We were engaged with preparations for our swearing-in the next day, so there was no breathing space. Beyond that, however, I was unable to charge my phone until the evening when the generator was turned on. So, it was with joyful expectation that I picked my phone and dialled the IPO at about 7 p.m. two days after I left Lagos.

"Hello, Benita," he said as he picked up the call.

"Hello sir, I am sorry…"

"Why has it been impossible to reach you? I have been trying your number since last night."

"My battery ran down and…"

"I am sorry, I have bad news for you… your friend is dead."

I took my phone away from my ear and looked at it like it was the face of the IPO. "I am sorry, what did you say...?"

"Your friend Halima died last night," he said more firmly this time. My scream drew the attention of everyone around the Block C hostel I was posted to, and at least five girls ran to me to find out if I was alright. I broke down in tears and must have cried for almost ninety minutes before I cleaned my face and dialled the IPO again, first to be sure that I heard correctly and if so, hear how that could have happened within forty-eight hours of my absence.

Although he was not at the station, the report he got was that Halima had tried to escape from the police station on Tuesday while I was on my journey to Kano.

"Halima was given the opportunity to take a shower at the back of the station. It is an open space because the bathroom in the female wing is bad. Because there was no female officer on duty on that day, she was left in the company of other ladies who raised the alarm when she tried to make away. When our men got there, she was climbing the fence. They warned her that they would have no choice than to shoot her if she failed to stop but she ignored them and went on trying to scale the fence. They fired shots at her, and she fell back into the station head down. She was said to have died on the spot. I am so sorry for your loss, but we will ensure that this is thoroughly investigated. In fact, the two officers who fired the shots are now in custody and..."

That was the last I heard of everything he said. The thought on my mind was Halima's warning that she was afraid for her life and how frightened she was the last time I saw her. I looked at my phone and I heard the IPO shouting "hello, hello" from the other side, exhausted and totally distraught at the reported death of this poor girl who had become like a sister to me in the few months that we spent together. I hung up and switched off my phone at once. I was sure that I would get back to ask more questions about how my beloved Halima died but at this moment, I needed to clear my head. I walked towards my hostel, tears flowed down my cheeks and blinded my eyes like drops of rain as flashes of moments Halima and I lived together enveloped my mind. Now, she was gone forever. How it happened, I would never be able to tell for sure.

IV

The Law is an Ass

"***With profound respect to this honourable court***, My Lord, I am disappointed in my learned friend on the other side for the idea of this suit. I consider it a total waste of this court's precious time and an unacceptable abuse of court process for counsel to file this suit when the precursory arbitral procedure, prescribed by the contract, has not been explored," Yusuf Abdulrahman, Senior Advocate of Nigeria said, his whole being trembling with anger.

He was addressing Justice Bintu Adewoye of the Federal High Court sitting in Abuja. The matter at hand regarded the termination of a construction contract between Leslie Plc., a multinational manufacturing company, and one Alhaji Saliu Muktar. Justice Adewoye was a no-nonsense judge who did not entertain unnecessary emotions in her court, and every lawyer, including members of the inner bar, tried not to cross the lines – hence Abdulrahman could not unleash his wrath on the junior lawyer as he would have wanted.

Ordinarily a man of fierce temper, the younger lawyer on the other side would have cursed the day he decided to become a lawyer, had the silk been given the opportunity to dress down someone he considered to be overzealous or outrightly incompetent. But no lawyer spoke condescendingly to another lawyer before this particular judge – no one.

Justice Adewoye lifted her head from the notes she was taking and opened her mouth to speak but then changed her mind. She shifted her glance, then looked straight at the senior advocate, biting the tip of her pen.

"Permit me, Your Lordship, to read from Article 6(2) of the agreement that governs this business relationship," Abdulrahman said, fixing a permanent glance on the judge, who was busy trying to fix her rimmed glasses more securely.

"Proceed, learned silk."

"Much obliged Your Lordship." Abdulrahman flipped through a bunch of files on the table before him, found a particular document, nodded with satisfaction and read:

> *All disputes and differences between the Parties hereto arising out of or in connection with this Agreement whether during the term hereof or after termination or breach shall in the first instance be referred to and settled under the Rules of Arbitration of the International Chamber of Commerce by one or more arbitrators appointed in accordance with the said Rules. The venue of Arbitration shall be New York...*

With this provision in the agreement, My Lord, it is inconceivable that my learned friend would initiate proceedings on behalf of the plaintiff in this honourable court. Thank you, my Lord," the senior advocate concluded, simultaneously taking a bow and taking his seat immediately after.

The judge sat upright, adjusted her glasses once again and addressed the counsel to the plaintiff, Barrister Tolu Alade, a zealous young man who had started his own practice a little over three years earlier.

"Mr. Alade, what do you have to say about this?"

"My Lord, we approached the court because of the difficulties my client currently contends with. The agreement provides that each party must fund the cost of the arbitration procedure in New York. The inconsiderate, arbitrary and oppressive termination of the contract by Leslie Plc. has rendered my client financially unstable and unable to fund such a journey at this time. So, to ensure that the course of justice is served, we reckoned that the option of approaching the national courts was best. This is why we are before this honourable court, My Lord."

After listening to these arguments, Justice Adewoye took about fifteen minutes to ponder the matter and then delivered a ruling which sent the parties to the International Court of Arbitration in New York.

"Parties can return to this court after a decision has been taken at the arbitration court," the learned judge pronounced, hit the gavel and rose for the day.

Barrister Alade felt the pronouncement of the court was a real kick in the teeth. He knew from the outset that he stood on very weak legal grounds, but he planned on playing on the emotion of the court by drawing attention to the penury of his client, a situation which he wanted to prove was imposed by the company's termination of the contract after his client had already taken bank loans and invested nearly all his livelihood.

Rulings that made him look incompetent like this detracted from the reputation he was trying to build for himself. This really broke his heart, even more than the misfortune of his client who would, by this ruling, have to look for money to fund a trip to New York.

A very brilliant young man by every standard of the word, two flaws – an uncompromising spirit premised on self-confidence and an obstinate lack of empathy – periodically impeded his progress. The latter was why inviting the court to consider the poverty of his client would surprise anyone remotely acquainted with this openly egoistic advocate. Alade, in promoting himself as a principled lawyer, hardly contemplated compromises or entertained "weak emotions." So, it was curious that he sought the understanding of the court while hanging on a completely extra-legal point.

He filed this case on behalf of Muktar who had secured a contract for the construction of a new production line for Leslie Plc. in Gadu, one of the major districts of Borno State. As is usual with such contracts, Muktar was expected to have executed a percentage of the job before getting an initial sixty per cent payment from the company. So, he approached the Trust Bank for a facility with a two-year tenure and was on the verge of mobilising to site when a terse correspondence from the company announced its decision to call the project off.

> *We consider this to be an unsafe investment given the current level of insecurity around the state. Management is therefore, forced to invoke the provision of Section 4(a) of our agreement with your organisation to the effect that parties are at liberty to cancel the contract by reason of any force majeure. We regret the inconvenience that this decision might cause your company and look forward to working with you in future.*

The letter, signed by Ali Musa, Executive Director, Finance and Administration for the company read.

Muktar was shaken. He had spoken with the same Ali, who was his classmate at the University of Maiduguri, the previous day and no hint had been given about this misfortune that just hit him. After the initial shock and consideration of what he should do, he called his old school mate who promised him that the cancellation was likely to be reversed in a few months. He explained that the company needed to reassess its investment in violent-prone areas across the north and that Gadu was a location that didn't have as much of the risks that the company feared.

"It had to be revoked in the interim, but we will revisit it all soon, so relax," his old classmate assured then.

Days however rolled into weeks, months and years without any review of the cancellation. His other friends advised Muktar to take legal action against the company, but Ali's assurances stopped him from considering this until years after the event, when it dawned on him that all the efforts at a peaceful resolution were producing no results. By this time, interests had accrued over the part of the principal he couldn't return immediately after the cancellation of the contract, and his residence which he had offered as collateral for the loan facility was about to be taken over by the bank. Friends and family, some of whom had advised him to pursue the peaceful option initially, now started to talk about going to court. It was at this point that one of Muktar's friends, Saliu Adejoh, introduced Alade.

Adejoh and Alade had lived in the same compound for close to three years, but the former knew little about the lawyer other than his loud, idealistic opinions. These opinions, which painted him as the ideal Nigerian iconoclast, were predictable whether it was the landlord who incurred his wrath or the government that introduced a policy that could impede on the liberty of the people in any form.

"He is a radical and I am sure he can get justice for you from the courts. The guy na no-nonsense person," Adejoh told Muktar the night before he arranged a meeting between prospective client and lawyer. Muktar was in any case the beggar who had no choice. In his financial state, he could hardly feed his family of four, let alone pay any high-profile lawyer. So, although he sensed a red flag in Alade's boisterous declarations of his erstwhile accomplishment, his lean pocket left him with no choice than to accept the thirty-five-year-old lawyer, warts and all.

But Alade was a brilliant advocate. Were he more patient and teachable, only the sky would limit his career. Smart, studious and blessed with the rare gift of identifying holes in the arguments of others, this young man was made for the law profession. As a matter of fact, by the time he was two months as an associate in the firm of Abiro and Co., where he cut his professional teeth, his talent stuck out like a piece of diamond, Mr. Olaleye, who was head of chambers at the time ensured that Alade made the research team in most of their cases, after which he joined the litigation team and got a few opportunities to represent clients. But pride soon got a hold of him. He started to see himself as the latest star in town, he disrespected many of his seniors in the firm and was soon returned to the back bench. He also showed himself to be utterly unreasonable. Alade saw no sense in the opinion of his seniors for settlement of cases out of court.

"You guys are just being lily-livered. We will win this case in court if we dare, I don't know why you want to chicken out," he would argue on occasions when settling out of court was contemplated. With this behaviour, his exit from the firm was a matter of time. That moment came five years into his tenure at Abiro and Co. Barrister Tolulope Alade, as he loved to call himself started A, L and D Associates with the tagline: *Lawyers for the people*.

Curiously, the tagline brought cases into A, L and D, in spite of its contradiction with the disposition of the principal of the chambers. Alade would ordinarily not bend over backwards for anyone, but he cashed in on the emotions of clients and their opponents to win cases, and in some cases, settled out of court. While he maintained a personality, which gave no concessions in his private life, he employed the instrumentality of the law to pawn on the emotions of susceptible people. That sentimental side of Muktar and the state of his finances lured him into choosing to go with this young lawyer.

As soon as Justice Adewoye hit the gavel after ruling on the SAN's application, Muktar asked his lawyer: "What are we going to do now?"

"Give me a minute sir," the lawyer responded and started to pack his books.

"I don't think we have time o. We need to decide on what to do."

"I know sir, I just need some time to think."

At that moment another lawyer about his age moved

close to him and whispered in his left ear: "The Learned Silk would like a word with you outside."

"What silk?" Alade replied, barely able to hide his irritation. He had an unhidden disdain for the senior advocate rank and the sense of entitlement that came with it, and the thought that anyone could summon him on the strength of being a senior advocate was nauseating. "Please, tell him I am not in the mood to speak with anyone," he fired at the other lawyer and resumed the packing of his books.

A couple of seconds later, he felt a light tap on his shoulder. Now, he was really infuriated and was going to give whoever it was a piece of his mind when he turned back to see the six-foot senior advocate standing behind him. Alade, in spite of himself, was dumbfounded.

Before he could find his voice, Abdulrahman offered: "Good afternoon, Mr. Alade. Good afternoon, Mr. Muktar," he leaned over to extend his greetings to the plaintiff.

"Emm, emm, good afternoon sir," Alade said, his lips shaking like leaves in the morning breeze, as he bowed his head and shook the hand Abdulrahman had extended to him.

"Can we step aside for a few minutes? There is something I want to talk to you about."

"I ... I am sorry sir, but can we please talk right here? I don't want to do anything without my client's knowledge."

"I understand that, but this should be a talk between

two lawyers, we can brief our clients later. As you can see, I don't have my client here…"

"With due respect, sir, we obviously operate in spectacularly different ways, I will respectfully request that we just talk here."

"Okay then, if you insist. I wanted to offer an amicable way out of this situation we have on our hands. I know that things aren't really good for your client and I wonder what we stand to gain from going back and forth on the matter. So, here is my offer, I can speak with my clients to give your client two new contracts as a form of settlement. They may not have the same value, but your client's loss won't be as colossal as it currently is. Everyone can go home and put this behind us."

"Yes, please, I am in agreement," Muktar sprang up from his seat. "I am very happy with that."

At the moment, Alade realised the rashness of his decision not to speak privately with Abdulrahman. He cast a look of disapproval at his client, who took his seat, subdued.

"Thank you for the offer sir. If I can have your contact information, I will discuss with my client and get back to you as soon as possible sir."

"Oh, that's exactly what I would expect. I look forward to getting a call from you," the SAN said, handing over his business card to Alade.

There was a heated debate at the office of the lawyer, at the end of which he convinced Muktar and his family that the offer was an indication that the other camp was jittery and therefore, the offer was a worthless one.

"They know we have a good case, and there is no way we will get less than a two hundred-million-naira award as damages and the enforcement of the contract terms as we claimed. I do not think we should take it!"

In the end, they agreed that the lawyer should reject the offer and prepare for the arbitration. To assure Muktar of his confidence in the matter, Alade promised to fund the trip for the arbitration procedure.

Two months later, parties appeared before the arbitration panel in New York. As soon as the panel invited counsel for Leslie Plc., one of Abdulrahman's associates, he argued that the claimants had no case because the matter had become statute barred.

"…. The law provides that disagreements arising from business relationships like the one under discussion be brought before a court of law within six years, failing which the claimant would be deemed to have slept on his rights. The position of the law at the moment is that the allowance the claimant had to have instituted this case has elapsed and this matter is just a waste of everybody's time. I therefore urge the court to dismiss this complaint. Thank you."

Invited to provide his argument, Alade told the court that the time for the cause of action should be the consideration rather than the period the contract was awarded. He contended that his client had pursued an amicable settlement for a number of years with the company not exhibiting good faith, and that the cause of action should be centred around the period when these attempts to an amicable settlement broke down, rather than the point at which the contract was terminated.

In the end, the panel of three arbitrators entered judgement in favour of Leslie. They agreed with the company's counsel that the cause of action arose on the day the claimant received the letter of termination of the contract, and that even though he may have had legitimate claims, his right to any reprieve had been extinguished at the expiration of the six years from the accrual of the right of action.

"The situation would have been different if the claimant had commenced an action even in a court lacking jurisdiction. Time would have frozen on behalf of the claimant and the time spent in the wrong court would have been discounted. But what we have here is different. It is a situation where the claimant employed extra judicial means until the passage of his right of action. I am therefore of the view that the action of the claimant herein is clearly statute barred," the judgment of the arbitration court read.

Alade, distraught by the judgement and debt he incurred to take the journey to New York returned to seek a review of the judgment of the Court of Arbitration.

Abdulrahman rejected this argument on the strength that the Federal High Court and the Arbitration Court of New York were courts of concurrent jurisdiction.

"Need I remind Mr. Alade," Abdulrahman said, disgust written on his face, "that this implies that this Honourable Court does not have the jurisdiction to review the judgment of the Court in New York. He can only approach the Court of Appeal if he wishes."

Again, Justice Adewoye agreed with the senior advocate and advised the counsel for the claimants to approach the Court of Appeal if he thought he had a reason to pursue the case.

Tears flowed down Muktar's face uncontrollably as a wave of ideas ran through his mind concerning his next step. From what he heard in court; he could tell that there was no hope on earth that he would win this case even if the case gets to the Supreme Court. He cursed himself for not following his instinct when he first met his lawyer. The guy, in spite of his evident brilliance, was too heady and full of himself. "God will punish him for misleading me in all of this. This his pride and over confidence will be his end just as he has brought this sad end to me…" He cursed under his breath.

"Hello sir, I want to suggest that we proceed upstairs to the court of appeal. I am sure we have a case…"

Muktar wanted to speak, but his tongue was stuck in his mouth. He tried to lift his left arm with the intent to tell his lawyer that his latest suggestion smacked of madness, but his arm failed to respond. At that instant, Alade realised something was wrong with his client. He rushed at him to offer help, but Muktar fell from his seat.

Everyone in the court dashed to offer help. A laboured shriek rang through the small room from the back. It was from Aisha, Muktar's wife of thirty years, who was seated at the back and sprinting to see what remained of the lifeless body of her husband.

V

The Money or the Child?

Kehinde Olatunmi decided early in life that he was going to be rich or die trying. When he came to that decision at the age of twelve, he had no idea how this would happen, but he had seen enough in his young life to know that life without money was hell, and he was going to do anything to make his life and that of his children better.

Four years later, Kehinde concluded that the one person who could help him was Adigun, a commercial driver who was his late father's best friend. Adigun drove two vehicles for this purpose – an 18-seater bus and a Peugeot 505 car. The nature of engagement determined which of the vehicles he used, but one thing was obvious – he made a lot of money from his business.

It was also obvious that Adigun had his own problems – too many as a matter of fact. Between his three wives, there were at least twenty children, yet he was the comforter of every widow in their village. Stealing into the beds of countless women, sowing his wild oats and spreading the dividends of his labour to the chagrin of his helpless wives and children. Luckily for Kehinde, he wasn't going to depend on Adigun for money; he knew

Adigun had been a driver on the Ilorin route for years, so he planned on asking for his help to get a job in the city.

He had completed his secondary education with grades good enough to proceed into a higher institution, but there was no money. After one year of farming and menial jobs in the village, he secured admission into a part-time programme at the state polytechnic at Ilorin. The idea of a part-time programme was to allow him work and attend lectures three evenings of the week and all day on Saturdays for three years for an Ordinary National Diploma (OND). So, early one morning, he went to the car park to speak with his father's friend encouraged by the blessing of his widowed mother.

"*E kaaro* sir," he said, prostrating in the traditional Yoruba way.

"Ah, *omo meji. Kaaro, ile nko? Mama e ati aburo e nko*?" The driver responded, asking after his mother and sister.

"Alafia sir."

"Hope no problem?"

"No sir, I came to talk to you about something."

"Oh, oya come here," he took Kehinde by the arm and led him to a row of benches where they both sat down to discuss.

Kehinde told his father's friend that he had secured admission into the state polytechnic and he would need a job to sustain himself while in school. Adigun was delighted at the news and after scratching his head for a while decided on what to do. The only person he could call for help was his big policeman friend. He told Kehinde to give him a moment, picked up his phone and went to call the policeman who promised to help him out. He returned to Kehinde brimming with smiles.

"Our prayers have been answered," he told Kehinde, who leapt in excitement and prostrated again.

"*A dupe sir, e pe fun wa sir.*"

"Amin o. But you must come to Ilorin this morning. As soon as I load my car, we will go and come back together. Let me take you to the man who will help, he wants to meet you." He said to Kehinde, who had no problem with the proposition.

A little over two hours later, Adigun's Peugeot 505 car was full with three other passengers, and they were on their way to the state capital. It was a smooth and uneventful journey that lasted ninety minutes. Throughout the trip, Adigun regaled Kehinde with stories of how good his father had been, the things they did together as children in the village, how his death had been an irreparable loss to him and how the family should not hesitate to come to him for anything.

He dropped off his other passengers at the garage and then proceeded to the home of Chief Superintendent of Police, Olade, who had promised to help him give Kehinde a job.

Olade worked at Division H in the central part of the city. They had become acquainted fifteen years earlier when his passengers turned out to be criminals. The policeman, who led a stop-and-search team positioned just before the border of the city, had flagged Adigun down at their checkpoint. Just as the driver applied the brakes, his passengers opened the doors, leapt out of the car and took to their heels. The policemen were too dumbfounded for a quick response. Before they could aim, focus and shoot, the passengers had fled deep into the bush. A pursuit wasn't an option with the potbellies of the policemen in Olade's company. They lamented for a few seconds before consoling themselves that they at least had the driver in their custody.

"On your knees," one of the policemen turned to Adigun in anger.

He raised his hands in surrender. "I no know them o, abeg. I just carry them for park," he fell on his knees and shouted, looking into the eyes of the policemen, one after the other.

The Inspector asked one of his men to handcuff the driver and put him in the back seat of the police van.

Adigun realised the extent of the trouble he could be in when as the policemen started to unpack one of the bags in the trunk of his car, two shotguns and several rounds of ammunition were brought out. Next was a wrapper dripping with blood and ten different types of mobile phones.

The eyes of the policeman brightened when after removing the wrapper, his hand touched a bundle of money. Excited, he dug deeper and unveiled layers and layers of cash. Their luck got better when they realised that the second bag was filled with money too. At the last count, their harvest for that day was in the excess of ten million naira. This left Olade in such a good mood that he asked his boys to immediately uncuff the driver, after which he listened to his story, exchanged numbers with him and blessed him with one hundred thousand naira.

Adigun, of course, counted himself lucky and felt indebted to the inspector. He knew very well that if he had not been favoured, the policemen could easily have killed him off or arrested him in connection with whatever offences his fleeing passengers had committed. He realised that the money they found would have become too difficult to explain if he was arrested, and the most likely option would have been his summary execution and disposal. He thanked his stars that he fell into the hand of a rare and good policeman like Olade and vowed to stay in touch with him, especially as insurance for the usual scuffles between drivers and policemen in that city.

He would, however, eventually discover that they had a mutual need for each other. The next time they spoke was just one week after the checkpoint incident. Adigun was about to retire to his room in the village when his phone rang, he was shocked to see who it was.

"Ah, Oga, good evening…" he started.

"Where are you, Adigun?"

"I dey village sir, you need me?"

"I want you to do something for me by 8 a.m. tomorrow. You must come o!"

Adigun cursed under his breath. He had thought of taking the next day off work but with the man instructing him this way, he had no choice but to go.

"Do you hear me? Meet me at Division H," the policeman said, hanging up without awaiting a response.

Like an angry but helpless goat, Adigun went to sleep, woke up early and was at the state capital the next morning. Before he arrived, Olade had called at least three times. They agreed to meet at the filling station some five hundred metres from the police station.

It turned out that the Inspector needed Adigun to travel to a boundary community from where bags of rice were smuggled into the country. They travelled all day, and when they got back at night, they drove straight to a massive building where the policeman's wife plied her trade. It was a big open hall where assorted foodstuff was piled up to the roof. There was beans, garri, and rice. Three young men were waiting to offload the consignment and they were done in no time.

"Adigun, you cannot return to the village tonight, so my boys will take you to the place you will sleep," Olade said. He handed him fifty thousand naira, thanked him for his assistance, hopped into a waiting Toyota Hilux and was driven away.

For the next fifteen years, they collaborated on many illegal endeavours, including the transportation of stolen goods, rescuing kidnappers from police custody and all sorts – the bond between Olade and Adigun had become so strong that it was no problem for him to request that his policeman friend who had now risen to Chief Superintendent of Police (CSP) provide part-time employment for his late friend's son.

"Adigun, Adigun, how are you my brother?" Olade welcomed his guests into his living room.

"I dey well, Oga. How body?" Adigun responded, and thereafter introduced his companion to the policeman. He told of their relationship, and of Kehinde's father and twin's untimely deaths.

"Now, the boy wan go school but money is not much, so please my oga, help us."

Olade said there was no problem.

"I like the boy the moment I set eyes on him and I will give him a job. I will also let him stay here. He can go to school from here, no problem at all," he assured Adigun. They agreed that Kehinde will be back in two weeks in preparation for school resumption.

Moving in with the Olades was like a divine arrangement for the teenage Kehinde, who soon started to see the police officer as his model. In their home where he stayed in a boys' quarters, nothing was lacking. He worked at the shop during the day, went to school at evening and weekends. Kehinde did well in school and soon became

Olade's favourite at home. The policeman was impressed that he could depend on Kehinde for feedback on the shady practices of workers in the food store and soon incorporated him into his shady deals with Adigun. In fact, on days when the assignment did not need police covering, he let Kehinde and Adigun go do the job.

He also rewarded Kehinde handsomely. The boy lacked nothing in school and always had enough to send to his mother and sister in the village. By the time he concluded his National Diploma, he already had an idea of how to achieve his old dream of becoming rich. All he wanted was to join the police force.

On his return from one of their rice smuggling trips one evening, Kehinde approached the policeman with a request.

"Emm, daddy," he started, scratching the back of his head, "Please I want to talk to you about something..."

Olade turned back in expectation. The boy always had juicy tales about the goings-on in the shop so, the policeman was also ready to hear him out. "What is it Kehinde?"

"Emm, daddy, please I want to join the police..."

"Huh?" the older man said tipping his head forward like he needed the young man to whisper what he just said into his ears. "I don't understand, where is that coming from?"

"I have been thinking about it, sir, I just love the job—"

"See, it's late and I am sure you are also tired, let's talk about this in the morning, okay? Goodnight."

This conversation went on for a couple of weeks during which Olade's disposition went from outright rejection of the idea, to his insistence that Kehinde continue his education and a final consideration of the benefits that could accrue from having someone from under his roof in the police force in the future.

Late one evening, he sent for Kehinde and asked him to sit down.

"I have been thinking about this your plan to join the police since you are serious about it. I think there is an opportunity we can explore."

"Thank God! Thank you, sir," Kehinde said leaping up from his seat in excitement. The next minute, he was on his knees thanking the CSP.

Olade ignored him. "The only problem is the opportunity is for secondary school certificate holders, so, your National Diploma will not count."

"I don't mind at all, sir. I don't mind," Kehinde said throwing himself on the floor before his benefactor. "*E se* sir. Thank you very much, sir."

Olade included Kehinde's application as part of the presidential approval for every state command to recruit hundred indigenes of each state into the police force. He also ensured that he was posted to one of the police stations under the zone he headed. As far as he was concerned, Kehinde, a young man he had grown so fond of, would remain under his tutelage for a few more years. He arranged for Kehinde to be posted to Araromi Division where Bambo, another protégé of his was Division Police Officer. Kehinde, being a proper village boy understood very well that any river that forgets its source would soon dry up. He was at Olade's service anytime the SP needed him, and it did not matter how lowly the task was.

Nevertheless, he knew that with time, he would have to devise the plan and strategy to attain his dream without hampering loyalty to the boss. This he was prepared to do, even to the point of subservience. He also had no trouble serving two masters, although life was made easier by the fact that his DPO reported to DCP Olade.

ASP Bambo, his DPO, was happy to have the Zonal Commander's boy in his care. For once, he was sure he had someone he could trust to execute extra tasks diligently and report back with honesty. Honest feedback was becoming an increasing rarity amongst recruits. He could only hope that the new boy wouldn't get influenced by the money mongers who now thronged the force. He decided to enjoy the boy's loyalty for as long as it lasted. So, on the days that Olade did not require the services of Kehinde, he made sure he had him at the major checkpoint under his command and Kehinde never failed, not once.

On one of those occasions when he was pressed for money, he had gotten Kehinde to plant a bullet in one man's car. Kehinde, dressed in his uniform, flagged down the car for a free ride at 10 a.m. Two kilometres after, he alighted from the car – his benefactor did not know that a bullet had been dropped in his car. He hadn't travelled another kilometre when he ran into a police checkpoint manned by people who already knew where to look for the contraband. They promptly found it and dragged the man to the police station. The illiterate businessman was threatened with everything including court action, but the matter was settled after he parted with one million naira, which was double what the DPO needed on this particular day.

On another occasion, Kehinde's patrol team arrived at an accident scene where a vehicle had somersaulted multiple times before landing in a gorge nearby. The policemen immediately set to work when they heard the weak cry of a child from the car. The Inspector in charge led his team towards the car to first rescue the child and then look out for the parents. As they got closer to the car, they saw notes of cash flying around in the harmattan breeze of the afternoon. That made them more curious, but it took just a few more steps towards the car before they discovered a bag of money about 200 metres from the car, apparently flung out during the incident. Impulsively the four of them, including the Inspector rushed at the bag like the waves of a violent wind. When money is involved, seniority usually takes the back seat with policemen and only when they picked up the bag did the most senior man bark at the others to take a step back.

"Kehinde, pick this bag up for assessment, oya, you two follow me," the inspector said, moving towards the car with the other two police officers grudgingly moving in tow.

But what they saw at the back of the car was another miracle they didn't expect. It was the Inspector who first shouted: "Wow, what is this?" The two constables with him rushed forward.

Beside the child who was strapped by a seat belt was another Ghana-must-go bag of money. The Inspector quickly looked to see if Kehinde has finished the assignment and started pulling out the bag by himself seeing the only one he could trust of his team members was still busy. He looked at the faces of the two men with him and shook his head, these were not people he could trust. He suspected that already, wads of notes would have found their way into the pockets of these officers and wondered why trust had become so rare. He chose to drag the bag out all by himself and wait for Kehinde to come back. While struggling with the bag, he asked one of his subordinates to bring the child out of the car and it was only then that he noticed a man whose head was slumped on the dashboard on the driver's seat. Kehinde arrived as he pulled the bag out of the car.

"Oya, Kehinde, take the bag. You two, come and lift the child up. The child go need urgent medical care," he said in pidgin.

Kehinde, already dragging the bag heard what the Inspector said, he stopped and looked back, confusion on his face.

"Inspector, you wan carry the child?"

"Oh yes, we fit save am, at least."

"But you no think say people go trace who him parents be. After that dey fit dey ask for the money wey dem carry and everyone go know say na we carry the baby."

The Inspector trying to piece it all together gave Kehinde a blank look as did the other two officers.

"So…." Inspector started throwing his hands in the air.

"I suggest we pack the money and leave these people here. If God love dem, help will come for them, if not, na their luck be that, no be we be God. But na you go decide, Oga."

The inspector stayed motionless for a minute or two. He thought about how true what Kehinde said was. If they took this baby to the hospital, questions would be asked about the parents and there was a chance some people would know that they had money inside their car. *That would turn the lights on us unless we just kuku turn the money in now*.

"I'll go with you Kehinde, let us leave them. God go help them," he said with finality and beckoned on his subordinates to follow him.

They dragged the bag of money to their van and headed towards the house of the DPO, where they would count the money, lock it up in the safe room, and return to the station to tell the boss of their big catch. They would then wait for their individual share after the zonal head and two other DPOs in the zone may have gotten theirs.

As he sat in the van, the Inspector marvelled at the haul they had for the day and thanked God for the opportunity. His mind drifted to Kehinde and his suggestion.

How on earth did he get that kind of idea? This boy may not be what we think he is after all o. Now, I know we really need to be careful with him. There are no saints among them, he thought, as he rested his head on the door of the van.

VI

Once Upon a Night

Phillips shifted uncomfortably in his seat. His eyes turned left, right and left again to see if there was any familiar face in the room. He nodded his head in relief, realising that it would be impossible for anyone to pick out his face in the dimness of the space he sat in.

Nevertheless, unable to control his unease, he brought a phone out from his breast pocket to see if he had missed any calls. He had put his phone on silent mode when he came in here in company of Jide, about thirty minutes earlier, assured of the fact that he had taken the last phone call for the night. Again, a tentative sense of satisfaction enveloped him. All things seemed to be working together, he thought to himself.

He took a sip of his *sex on the beach*, the cocktail he had chosen in preparation for his mission for the night, even as he wondered if he was doing the right thing. On more than one occasion this night, he had been hit by a bout of guilt and some foreboding, such that he had at one point contemplated aborting the whole plan. But he dismissed the thought before it could even take root and germinate into an impediment. *Nothing under the heavens will be able to stop me tonight*. There were two reasons why he could not even consider backtracking, he reminded himself.

His friends, who put him up to this, would never forgive him for developing cold feet at the last hour. Secondly and most importantly, this was the best way to deal with Ada, that bitch of a wife who led him into the temptation of bowing to the pressure of friends and visiting this kind of venue shortly after his marriage.

"This woman has taken me for granted enough and the time has come for me to show her that I can do what other men do," he muttered, letting out a long hiss which ended in a frown that revealed his utter contempt for the woman on his mind.

It had been two years since they first met at the Iyana Ipaja, Lagos orientation camp of the National Youth Service Corps (NYSC). And it was lust at first sight, at least from where Phillips stood. He had gone to the orientation camp to interview corps members as part of the human resources team of a multinational fast-moving consumer goods company where he worked. It was the tradition of blue-chip companies to seek out graduates with good degrees and admit them into an elite graduate trainee programme which prepared them for roles in the future of these organisations. This was where the fortune of meeting the drop-dead gorgeous Ada fell on him. Although a sucker for beauty, which he unrepentantly defined as "height not less than 5 feet 8 inches, bust in the C and D cups with sizes between 36 and 38, and a body in the 12-14 range." Phillips nursed no thoughts about girls until this young lady happened on him and his team.

On arrival at the camp, fifty corps members from across the country were already seated under a cream canopy outside the small meeting room, which the NYSC officials had prepared for the interview. The team immediately moved into the room and commenced the process. It went on routinely until Ada sashayed in midway into the process.

Even in the unattractive full NYSC uniform that she had to wear for occasions like this, this daughter of Enugu-based medical doctors shone like a star on a dark night. Ada stood at about five feet, eight inches, her skin was soft and light-complexioned, with curves in all the right places. When she greeted the three-man interview panel, she accompanied it with a bright smile that melted their hearts.

While the two other panellists nodded in acknowledgment of Ada's greeting, Phillips took in the impressive figure before him. His gaze sent a quick message through his whole being, he readjusted himself on his seat as he stole further glances at the elegant piece of work.

Adept at his appreciation of good looks, he had taken all the details in a moment: long silky hair which hung past her shoulders, firm and full breasts. He licked his lips before he got jolted back to reality by the lead interviewer, Mr. Usman's offer of a seat to the young lady.

Ada took her seat with measured calmness offering an emphatic "thank you very much," and settled for the interview that went on for about fifteen minutes, during which Phillips was too entranced to ask any question at all.

He would discover during the interview that in addition to her beauty, Miss Obi was an embodiment of brilliance and intelligence, a combination which could cause every lover of good things some heart palpitations. That day he promised himself that he would give anything to unravel the mystery under the skin of this ravishing lady.

It turned out that Phillips did not need to lift a finger to get Ada on the shortlist for his company's NYSC intakes for that year. She outperformed every other applicant, gained a place without much ado, and resumed at the headquarters of the organisation in the Ikeja area of Lagos exactly three weeks after the interview at the orientation camp.

Having been acquainted earlier, Phillips swiftly positioned himself as the angel sent to help Ada navigate the everyday challenges of the company and the city of Lagos. Before long, they became an item, to the envy of men of similar lascivious appetites in their workplace. Their orientation camp acquaintance already handed Phillips the edge over them all. What was more, he made a huge impression of his kindness on Ada such that when he eventually asked to date her, the pathway was already clear.

He would pick Ada from the accommodation provided for members of the NYSC by the company every morning and drop her off after work. When he was not in town, he made it his duty to get one of his friends to fill in for him. He ensured that there was food for the young lady every lunch time and would every now and then, surprise her with a variety of things that she loved.

However, it didn't take too long before lover boy Phillips started getting irritated by no indications of expected dividend, despite his niceness. He had been with quite a number of girls in his life and some of them did not even wait for a formal relationship before letting him have a piece of them, but things were dragging on too long with Ada and it began to disturb him. Although, in the few weeks of knowing her, he saw her as a nice girl any man could consider for his future, but that was not his priority now. At just twenty-eight, he felt there was ample time to explore and scale up his body count to match up with Jide and his other friends.

Jide, his friend of over one decade was the one reason for his obsession with extremely beautiful girls, and this started two years after they became graduate trainees at the multinational where they both worked. They met when they were in 200 Level at the Public Administration Department of the University of Benin and had stuck together like Siamese twins since.

Over the years, Jide had become more like a brother to Phillips than a friend. As students in the University, they paid more attention to their studies than the ever-contending interest for socialising. At the end of their second year they were both at the top of their class and encouraged one another to maintain this. This advantage itself would draw many young ladies, but the boys had little association beyond the academic with the girls who swarmed round them like bees. For Phillips especially, the admonition of his mother on the dangers of getting distracted by the opposite sex rang in his head anytime his closeness to a girl was tending towards intimacy. He wanted to study, pass well and save the little money his mother sent to him to feed and buy the necessary supplies.

Five years down the line though, this disposition was dead and forgotten. The lives of the jolly friends had taken a dramatic turn. Having maintained their streak of brilliance until the very end, their exceptional degrees brought so many opportunities their way. In the end, they both chose to work in the same company, where access to money and opportunities caused the unleashing of the dragons within.

While the two of them had different ideas of what made a woman beautiful, no woman escaped their determination to make up for the years lost at the university. Frequently, they compared notes and admonished each other when they were “slacking”. This was the guiding philosophy at the time Phillips met Ada.

Given their history, Phillips discussed his growing impatience with his friend from whom he got nothing but sharp reprimands for getting carried away with the girl’s unusual beauty. He expressed doubts about the girl's claim that she was waiting for her wedding night for her first sexual experience, affirming that there was no way her cherry would not have been popped.

"Look, old boy, if the girl no wan do, abeg leave am. I think you have done enough good boy already," Jide had told him the last time her issue came up. Phillips gave thought to the matter as he drove home after dropping Ada off that night.

I really need to find a way out of the matter before this girl begins to think one is an idiot. Later that night, he arrived at a conclusion to put an end to his situation, no matter the cost.

The opportunity to take a go at it came after dinner at The Emperor's Place, a restaurant in Ikeja GRA, the following week. As they dug into their meals, sharing jokes and giggling, Phillips assured himself that the night of unveiling had finally come. On previous occasions when they had such outings, he would ask Ada whether they should retire to his place and on every occasion, she had replied in the negative. This evening, he was not going to give her the honour of turning him down. As soon as they got into his car, he would drive toward his home in Ogudu GRA and damn the consequence, he thought.

But the consequence was nothing the young man imagined. As he pulled out of the restaurant and turned left to hit Joel Ogunnaike Street, Ada expected another left turn that would lead them to Oba Akinjobi, and then on to Ikeja Under-bridge which would ultimately take them to Adeniyi Jones Street, where the company had secured two flats for all its corps members. That did not happen.

"Where are you heading to?" she asked, turning 180 degrees to get a good view of Phillips, as the latter took the right turn past Country Club to hit the popular Bank Anthony Street. It took about thirty seconds before the question sank in and by then, Phillips was approaching the traffic lights at the NITEL intersection. He stepped on the brakes; the car came to a stop just as the lights turned red. "I thought we should end the very pleasant evening at my home, Ada," Phillips said, taking his hand off the steering wheel and reaching for the blemish-free skin that Ada's short skirt revealed.

Ada's next action shocked him.

Just before his hand could reach its destination, Ada flung open the door of the car, took one second to see that it was safe to dash out and instantly shot out of the car, slamming the door behind her. Phillips had never been so confused in his life. He yelled for her, but the lights turned green. A cacophony of horns blared all around him, and in that moment, he had no choice than to drive on towards the Ikeja Military Cantonment before he could make a U-turn to see if Ada would be somewhere around Sobo Arobiodu or the adjacent Isaac John Street, having been hit by a sense of guilt at his own behaviour. His search was a wasted effort. He tried to call her to no avail and after having satisfied the urge to check the streets, Phillips knew there was nowhere else she would have gone but the corpers' residence.

He made his way to Adeniyi Jones, through the traffic on Oba Akinjobi into Kodesho Street, asking himself why he had gone through all this trouble. This was surely not the only girl he could be with. She was truly an outstanding beauty but was she worth this trouble, especially since she had blatantly refused to let him have his way?

As he turned his car into the compound, Ada called him. Philips took a contemptuous look at the ringing phone and the caller identity, contemplating whether to take the call or not. He resolved to take it.

"Hello, Ada," he spoke into the phone with subdued anger which melted away the moment he heard soft sobs from the other end.

"I am sorry, Phillips" Ada said, trying to suppress her emotion. "I am sorry for my behaviour, please forgive me, I promise…"

"Shh," Phillips interrupted her. "Where are you?"

"I am at home," Ada replied.

"Oh, great, please come out. I am outside in the car," Phillips said, now totally disarmed by the evident remorse of the young lady.

Within minutes Ada was in the car, apologising and promising that no such erratic display would occur again. To show how repentant she was, she asked to pack a change of clothes and follow Phillips home with the caveat that there would be no attempt at sex. She reiterated the story she had told Phillips countless times. How her mother and her own mother before her had gone to their husbands' houses as virgins. How her mother had taught her to remain untouched until the night of her wedding, and how she had sworn to her mother at twelve to remain a virgin and do anything, include losing a relationship, to achieve that.

This story had become tiresome for Phillips. Even though the emotional state he met Ada in had softened him up, he was not in the mood for any babysitting. He did not understand the fuss about remaining a virgin until her wedding night and how her ancestors had remained so chaste. He did not see how any of these should be his business and thought that since Ada was insisting on sticking to her guns, she could as well remain in her house.

"It is fine Ada. I think you should stay at home with your friends tonight. We can talk more about this tomorrow. I am happy that you are home and well."

Ada, head inclined on Phillips' shoulders took a real mushy look at him and asked: "Are you sure about this?"

Phillips nodded and planted a kiss on her cheek. "I should be on my way now, Ada, it's getting pretty late."

The next week were days of intensive contemplation for Phillips. He thought about how much he had tried to impress Ada, just to get into her panties. How none of what he had done could drop the girl's guard and Jide's counsel on letting her go.

He found himself tending toward Jide's advice. It just did not make sense to keep chasing after Ada, considering the number of beautiful girls who had succumbed to his charm. Yet there was something special about this girl that he could not put a finger on, all he knew was that he would give anything to have a moment in bed with Ada. Apart from being a beauty, the fact that she was a virgin was something he couldn't get over, he had never been with a virgin and nothing could ever be as fulfilling as having this particularly beautiful girl. Then, he thought about what the only impediment was – marriage.

So, if I choose to marry this girl now, she would be mine? What then stops me from marrying her? I have got everything a man needs to marry, and here is one hell of a girl that I do not want to miss, shouldn't I just consider marriage to her and propose?

These thoughts pre-occupied his mind for the next two weeks, at the end of which the idea of proposing marriage to Ada had taken firm root. The more Jide tried to dissuade him from the idea, which he felt was senseless and premature, the more resolute Phillips became.

At the end of the second week, he proposed marriage to Ada, who herself was dumbfounded, not having imagined that it could happen to her so soon. When she raised the issue with her mother however, she got all the encouragement she needed. Her mom, unapologetic of her determination to marry her first daughter off in a chaste state, felt that the earlier this happened the better.

In all of this, Phillips looked forward to the wedding night when he would finally make a woman of his beautiful bride. On the wedding day, he was confident that he had finally secured what seemed to be the most precious desire of his adult life – making Ada his own!

Preparatory to their honeymoon trip to the United Kingdom, scheduled for the day after the wedding, the couple checked into one of the highbrow hotels in Ikeja. Phillips prepared all of himself for the most important event of the day.

That night, he felt on top of the world. Although he could not say the pleasure of that night was anything near what he was used to, he confirmed that Ada was indeed a virgin and felt like he had won a prize for it! He hoped that the intimacy would get better, and he could teach his wife some new things in the days coming.

Unfortunately, things did not get better in the course of their two-week trip. Not only did he find sex with his wife uninspiring, but he was also disgusted by her laziness and blatant disinterest in learning how to please her partner. By the end of their first week in London, Phillips called Jide about the situation. After having a good laugh, for which Phillips almost hung up on his friend, he advised him to be more patient with his wife.

"We both know say this girl dey green. She can't just learn all those things you want her to do within this short period. I think you should give her some time, things will get better, okay? Just take it easy."

"Hmmm, okay bro, thanks mehn. I just hope things will change, I really just hope," Phillips said, hanging up.

But things did not get better, in fact, they got worse. Within three to four weeks of their return to Nigeria, Ada developed a fever, which persisted until they had to see a doctor. A barrage of tests was ordered but only one returned positive – pregnancy. This put even more stress on their marriage. The couple had planned to enjoy each other's company for one year before starting a family but now this had put a stop to it.

For a man who was already whining about the less-than-satisfactory coition with his wife, this unexpected pregnancy only made his life more miserable. It was that kind of round-the-clock, relentless misery that makes a man want to run away. It got to a head one week after the test result. Ada woke him up between 6.30 and 7 a.m. every morning with burps as loud as those of a drunken man trying to find his way home. It was a situation Phillips never got used to.

Fortunately, she had completed her youth service one week before they got married, they were awaiting feedback from another multinational she applied to, so, she had the liberty of staying at home at that moment. But madam called every other hour to complain about one thing or another. It was either a headache was threatening to kill her, or some cravings that no one around could satiate. At other times, it would be her legs and her tummy hurting so much that she wished they could be severed from her body, or some other strange complaints that made her husband contemplate just leaving town.

As if everything was a conspiracy to make life unbearable, doctors began to talk about Ada needing a caesarean section to deliver her baby. Scans had identified that the baby was in a breech position at twenty-eight weeks.

"But the baby is still just about 2.5kg, so there is every chance he might turn," the consultant gynaecologist told them on one of the visits they made together.

" Oh, not again," Ada let off a cry, which drew a smile from the doctor.

"It's nothing to worry about, Ada. There is a very big chance that the baby will turn before your next visit. So, let's not get agitated, alright?"

But the baby maintained its breech position at thirty-six weeks and at that point, doctors felt it was safer to bring out the baby before the mother fell into labour. The procedure went without incident and Phillips, despite all his disgust at the disruption the pregnancy had caused, was beside himself when he first saw his baby boy. His wife was still drowsy from the effect of the anaesthesia, so he had a long time to wait on her and the baby.

Mother and baby were released from the hospital one week after delivery. Phillips soon discovered that the birth of Joshua, their son, had brought a deeper wedge between him and his wife, systematically taking her attention away from him. You would have thought that having Joshua was the only reason she got married. For unfathomable reasons, Ada suddenly took her attention from him and his needs, and instead became increasingly devoted to their son.

He shook his head in sympathy for himself, considering all the deprivations he had endured at the hands of this woman, anger erupted in him against himself and how much he had condoned his wife's irresponsibility.

"Old boy, are you ready for tonight? The action is about to start," Jide jolted him back to the present with a gentle tap on his shoulder.

His heart skipped two beats. He noticed that there were four girls hovering around his friend. He took a quick look at the girls and saw that they were all in pieces of clothing that left little to the imagination.

Before he could say a word, Jide tapped him on the shoulder again, addressing two of the girls: "Cynthia and Eno, here is my friend, Phillips. You guys will be keeping him company tonight." He gave Phillips a knowing look, which further unsettled the latter.

Phillips lifted his finger to indicate he would like to have a private moment with his friend and the two of them dragged each other to a corner where the loud music in the room would drown their voices.

"See Jide, I am really nervous, what am I going to do with these two girls?" Phillips asked, anxiety written all over him.

"Shey you have started again, abi? Did we not discuss all of this?" Jide replied angrily. "You do not have to worry yourself about anything, they know what to do and will take charge once you get into the room we've arranged. All you need do is just relax and have fun, *hian*! Go and have a feel of what you have missed so much bro!" Jide shook his friend's hand with vigour.

Phillips eventually followed the lead of his escorts into one of the luxurious rooms on the second floor of the night club. Cynthia opened the door wide for Phillips to walk in, after which Eno followed. Cynthia, the taller of the two ladies then walked in, shut and bolted the door behind her. She turned to look intently at Phillips, the man totally at their mercy, and smiled broadly. He smiled sheepishly.

She took two measured steps and reached Phillips. They were about the same height and that really pleased her. Placing her hands on his shoulder, she drew a now totally enthralled Phillips close to her and planted a full kiss on his lips. She could feel his body shivering. She stopped kissing him for a moment, smiled at him once again and told him with all assurance: "Oga, just relax, you are in very good hands and we promise you a very memorable night. Isn't that so Eno?" Eno, who had all the while behaved like she was not present in the room, affirmed her partner's assertion with an emphatic "Absolutely."

Phillips looked on as Cynthia, obviously the team lead, pushed him on the bed and seeing him comfortably lying across, stepped back and undid her blouse. That move revealed a rich bosom that instantly caused Phillips' heart to race. The lady dropped to her knees and crawled towards Philips who lay like a log of wood. Suddenly, she turned back and waved her hand at Eno.

Eno, also having removed every shred of clothing hiding her spotless and curvy body, fetched the handbag she had placed on the table. Opening it, she brought out a lighter and two wraps. She lit the first one and handed it over to Cynthia who took one long drag, stood up on her feet and attempted to put it into Phillips' mouth. He pushed her hand away and that made Cynthia laugh very hard.

She handed the wrap to her partner, dropped onto her knees at the foot of the bed and started to undo Phillips' belt. She was still struggling with the object when Eno's incessant cough drew her attention. Cynthia stopped for a moment, looked back and saw Eno bending over.

"Eno are you okay?"

She got no reply, but the coughing seemed to get more intense and shorter by the second. And then, she heard a thud and saw that Eno had collapsed on the table in the room.

Now, really alarmed, she stood up shouting the name of her partner. Phillips himself, realising he might be in serious trouble, sat up. He wondered how he would explain this situation, searching his pocket for his phone so he could call Jide. Sweat poured from all over his body even though the air conditioning in the room was at the lowest temperature. As he dialled Jide's number a second time, wondering what kind of indulgence was preventing him from picking up, he saw Cynthia transform into a helpless jerk, naked, and running helter-skelter, her breasts bouncing ahead of her. He promised himself never to try this shit again if he ever found a way to avoid the impending disgrace.

That same moment, he woke up on his bed at home. But for the balls of sweat he felt on his forehead, nothing around him reflected the experience of the last few minutes. He looked to his left and found Ada sleeping peacefully, a disarming smile on her face, and to his left their baby lay in his cot. He looked up to the heavens and prayed quietly: "May I never find myself in that situation."

VII
Devil's Table

Stanley walked down the hallway behind the young man who received him at the door. His guide had introduced himself as Tony and bowed when Stanley offered to shake hands. The long hallway smelled like it had only recently been sprayed with several bottles of rich perfumes. Stanley, despite himself, was taken in by the calming effect of the fragrances. He took a deep breath in inhalation of the aroma; an almost palpable sense of freshness filled his entire being. He smiled for a moment before thinking to himself that this was the smell of the political class's abuse of the common man's trust, something he was determined to fight in his own little way.

He stopped abruptly as they walked into one of the adjoining rooms and took a fleeting, contemptible look around. He noticed the opulence dripping out of every item in the expansive room. Although he did not have any specific idea of the items of décor and furniture in the room, as he was not brought up to savour such vanity, he could tell that tons of money had gone into the furnishing, the moment his feet sank into the soft rug on the medium tone wooden floor.

Beyond the golden chandelier, which dangled in the middle of the room and made him wish that these politicians had hearts that were half as golden and considerate of the people, the only other thing that made sense to him in the room was a finely polished bookshelf that stood at the far right.

As he moved closer to the sitting area, which as far as he was concerned, was a confused and eccentric gathering of colours and shapes of furniture, he could cite titles of some Nigerian authors. That felt really odd. He never imagined these politicians read fiction, *or could this display just be an attempt to impress him? Whatever it is, they are bound to fail.*

"Come take a seat, sir. His Excellency will soon join you," Tony said.

He looked up at Tony who was walking into an inner room and muttered a reluctant "thank you."

Stanley sank into one of the couches in the room and wished in his heart that this governor would not waste his time. He was not in the mood to indulge any politician who got a kick out of keeping people waiting. Stanley looked at the clock on the wall, it was half-past eleven and a clear thirty minutes before his appointment with the governor.

"I'll give him the benefit of an extra thirty minutes after which, I am out of here," he muttered, drew the zipper of the sling bag housing the new MacBook Air 2020 he just got for winning the Nigeria Media Merit Award as

Best Investigative Writer in 2019 and brought out his copy of Toni Kan's *The Carnivorous City*.

He turned the book up, down, and up again, a smile on his face. It was the first time all day he'd felt any joy and he was ready to savour that moment, being almost sure that his meeting with the "overfed fool," who called himself the state governor, was sure to foul up his mood. He opened the novel having concluded that there was no need to live the predictably miserable time with the governor twice. *Let me just wait for it and enjoy this moment reading*.

Soni is missing. Three simple words that seemed as if a lifetime had been compressed into them, a lethal payload of pain and fear waiting to detonate and decimate. Those words shocked and calmed in equal measure, like a letter bearing bad news delivered long after its content had been made known, he read from the book.

Stanley closed the pages of the book and shook his head contemplatively. He hit the edge of the couch he was sitting on three times successively and muttered: "Chai, this guy can write."

He reread the opening paragraph, convinced that he was in for a delightful ride with this book. Just then, he heard footsteps coming out of the inner room, took his eyes off the door, and decided to concentrate on his reading.

"Good afternoon," he heard someone say, and looked up to see it was a clergy man dressed in a cassock.

His stomach churned with repulsion. He hated the sight of these hypocrite traders in divine cloak. *Why can't this one stay in the community bank where they fleece Nigerians of their hard-earned monies?* Ignoring the man of God, he noticed it was about five minutes to noon and went back to his book.

Stanley believed he had every reason to detest these charlatans who called themselves clerics. Not only was one of them said to be responsible for the untimely death of his father, but the same criminal in cassock also deceived his mother into marriage and duped her of the little fortune her husband left for her and their only son before dropping out of circulation like thin air. It was a loss that sent his mother into penury.

His father, Nobert Chukas, whose law practice in the city of Asaba thrived at that time had invited the prophet into their lives on the advice of his only surviving sister, Aunt Lovina. Lovina's counsel followed a bizarre dream his father had where he saw vultures eating from his head. Although not ordinarily given to dignifying the spiritual, this dream scared the life out of him. He talked to his sister who was a spiritual peddler and naturally presented a solution in Prophet Linus, an itinerant spiritualist who had been of service a couple of times.

Upon invitation, the spiritualist asked for three days to pray and fast. He came back after his retreat to say that one of the most prominent lawyers in the city was seeking the life of Mr. Chukas. He gave a list of procedures that would avert the impending evil and in fact, reverse it onto the attacker. In spite of himself, Nobert Chukas did all the prophet asked for and put the matter behind him, at least until two weeks later when Chief Agbas, the most prominent lawyer in the city and one who treated Chukas like a rival died in his sleep! The conclusion was that Agbas was the one who wanted the lawyer dead and for the seeming accuracy of the interpretation of his dream, Linus earned the stripe as the spiritual consultant of the family. He got so close that Mr. Chukas, though apathetic to any religion, consulted him on literally everything, including family issues he would not discuss with his wife. He went on to designate a part of the house for the prophet to stay anytime he was in the city.

Ten months after his first encounter with Linus, Nobert Chukas fell ill and was dead within one week. Upon his death, he left his wife, Abigail and their only child, Stanley, everything he owned, running into a few millions, to the chagrin of his only sister who started a fight with his brother's widow. Linus, having become an integral part of the family, sided with Abigail all the way and before long, found his way into her bed, got access to the family account and eventually made away with what Abigail quantified to be about three million naira.

Abigail would later tell her son of suspicions that this false prophet poisoned her husband and hypnotised her to get to the family resources. Since he heard this story, Stanley Chukas did any and everything within his power to expose what he saw as the unbridled hypocrisy of religionists in the country.

It was hard to blame the talented journalist. The death of his father and subsequent duping of his mother left them near penniless. Although she trained as a secretary, his mother was a full-time housewife when her husband lived, so, getting a job after she became a widow was difficult. She had no work experience, and no one was ready to employ a middle-aged starter.

She sourced for funds to start a textile business from her family members, but this didn't bring much more than what could pay for their accommodation, feed them and pay Stanley's way through school. Things only started to improve when he discovered his writing talent and began to send articles to the newspapers as a student in the university. One of them, *The National Independent*, offered him a job in his final year and he had remained with them till date.

"Good afternoon, China," he heard a gentle, nevertheless firm voice say. Stanley sprung to his feet in surprise. This was the governor himself standing right before him, hands outstretched. This scene was unsimilar to his contemplations, the governor had even called him by his nickname, which he acquired because of his communist views while in the university. Only a few people who knew him in school still called him that.

"How are you today, my dear friend?" Governor Koras asked.

“I am very well, Mr. Governor, thank you very much, sir.”

“That’s good to know. Please come with me,” Koras said, leading the way into the inner room he had emerged from.

The inner room led them into another big room, the size of the one he just left. The governor’s gesture disarmed him momentarily, but the journalist could not help his disgust at the level of waste in the Government House – the sheer size of this room, the expensive furniture and electronics and the massive air-conditioning. Just when he thought he had seen it all, the Governor turned into another room on his left and at that point, Stanley gave up. He discovered that this was a smaller room that could only take a meeting of three, but he noticed another door at the edge of the smaller room and that was where the governor headed, he followed.

At last, they arrived at an expansive dining room where three other people, including Tony, one stunningly pretty lady and another guy were seated. The three fellows rose as the governor stepped into the room and sat down at the wave of his hand: “Welcome back, Your Excellency,” they chorused.

The governor took the seat at the head of the table. He pointed to the seat to his left and asked his guest to “please sit”.

“Thank you, sir,” Stanley said.

"You are welcome, and I must say it is really good to finally put a face to the name," the governor said, following his comment with a burst of very hearty laughter that thoroughly embarrassed his guest.

"Let me introduce you to my team. I believe you have met Tony. He is my Personal Assistant, Domestic. The lady here is Adaora, she is my Personal Assistant, Special Duties, while John over there is my Personal Assistant."

Stanley waved hello at the three people on the other side of the table. He wondered why one man needed three personal assistants.

"I am sure you are wondering why I have three PAs, but this job is killing, my brother, and each of them does something that makes my life and governance easier."

"Hmm. Okay sir," Stanley responded.

"Anyway, let us have a meal after which we can talk about why I invited you."

Lunch went on for another forty-five minutes during which the governor tried to know more about his guest. He asked about family, work and his aspirations for the future. He congratulated him on the good job he did, which had garnered him some awards, and asked if he was ever interested in politics.

"Ah! No, Mr. Governor, not in this life, sir," Stanley said, his face suddenly wearing a frown that threw the governor into hysterical laughter.

"What is wrong with politics? Why are you so scared?"

"Can I be honest?"

"Absolutely, please."

"I am actually not scared. I am not just cut out for politics. I, with due respect, do not think it is meant for decent people. I am sorry but I mean no offence."

"Of course. None taken actually. I am just a bit curious at the logic of people like you who claim to want the best for the country but think politics is too dirty for them. Do you realise that the future of the country depends on politicians? So, if you leave it to the "dirty" people that you speak about, how is the country going to make progress?"

Stanley started to talk, but his host cut him off.

"It's fine, China. I'm sure … well, hopeful that you and I will have ample time to discuss politics in future. Can we talk about why I invited you?"

"Of course, sir. I wonder though, how you knew my nickname?"

The governor laughed. "You are funny, Stanley. You forget I am the governor of this state. I know everything!" Koras said, getting up from his seat, he pulled Stanley up by his hand and beckoned on his staff to come along. He walked along with them into yet another meeting room adjoining the dining room, sat on the only three-seater couch in the room and motioned to Stanley to sit by his side. His staff also made themselves comfortable.

"Not to waste your time further, I'll cut to the chase. Let me thank you for making time out to see me. I saw the article you wrote about us and it's a very biting one, but I imagine that it's because you do not have proper information about what we are doing. So, I thought to thank you for having an interest in us to start with, and then offer an opportunity for you to take a tour of three senatorial districts to see one legacy project in each of them and give us your impression on your return. You do not even need to do any story when you get back. I just would love for you to see things yourself. That is my proposal."

"Oh, wow! Thank you for the invitation but it's not the kind of thing I do. However, I will think about it and get back to you."

"That is fair enough. If you can oblige us, please think about it. Adaora here will let you have her number. In fact, three of you should exchange numbers with him. So, when you make up your mind, Adaora will coordinate your movement. Kindly let her know whatever you need. I really do hope we can do this together. And let me explain something, I am not involving my media people in this because I don't want any drama. So, whatever we agree to do would be with these personal staffers of mine."

"We shall see how it goes."

"Great then. Enjoy the rest of the day," the governor shook hands with him and turned to leave the room. He stopped abruptly and addressed Stanley.

"I forgot to give you my number," he brought out an already signed business card, took out his pen and marked one of the numbers on the card. "This is my private number. Call me anytime. If I don't pick, send a text. I sure will call you back."

Stanley reluctantly exchanged phone numbers with Governor Koras' staffers. He wasn't keen on the offer the governor made to him and would have no need to call any of these characters, he thought as he walked out of the meeting room. Tony and Adaora walked him to the car park and watched him drive off.

He drove into the premises of *The National Independent* where he worked as a weekend editor and columnist, thinking about how mistaken he was about the governor. The article the man referred to had speculated that he was a laid-back, wannabe intellectual who had turned the fortune of their state backwards. But this afternoon's meeting gave him a totally different perspective. Although he still couldn't tell how much milk of compassion flowed in the governor, that meeting convinced him of Koras' intellectual capacity, so things were probably not as bad as he had thought.

The invitation to visit the government projects was a temptation Stanley battled to avoid for the next one week. Mindful of the saying that a sheep that moves with the dog would soon start to eat faeces, he had held onto the principle of not getting too close to politicians since he started his journalism career. However, this was an opportunity to verify some of the work that the present state administration laid claims to. Such were the arguments advanced by his colleague editors at *The*

Independent's stable when he told them about the offer. Although he was usually wary of counsel from the Daily Editor, Donnie, who he knew to be an insatiable money-monger and influence- craver, the guy seemed to make some sense when he countered Stanley's argument that a true journalist had to grab every opportunity to learn more about anything. As simple as that statement was, it bore an indisputable truth about the whole essence of journalism.

As he laid on the bed, exactly one week after his meeting with the governor, Stanley probed himself to determine what his hesitation was about. He had been a man of ethics throughout his career, refusing to be swayed by any kind of distraction or compromise, so what made this different? He wondered what risks would be involved if he decided to take up the offer from which he was bound to gain a lot of insight. He decided to call Adaora to tell her he would accept the challenge. *And even if they have any undesirable plans, they will meet me here rock solid.*

Things moved very fast after he spoke with Adaora in the morning. Arrangements were made for him to travel the following week and as the governor had said, no one on his media team was involved in the plans. Stanley was driven in an unmarked SUV from the Government House. He also had two men of the Mobile Police Unit attached to him to provide security, they travelled in a Toyota Hilux patrol van. Within a week, he was taken through the Agricultural, Independent Power and Vocational Training projects initiated by the government.

He was in fact impressed with the ideas of these projects. They further showed the governor as a thinking person who understood development. However, he was worried about a few things. The first was the amount of money the government was spending on the projects. He felt that rather than being sole investors, the government should have sought for private investors to guaranty the sustainability of these projects. The government has always failed at doing business in Nigeria, because most of those who work for them see these ventures as part of the national cake. He was also concerned about how much local content was engaged in the projects.

For instance, I noticed that we have foreigners who recently migrated to Nigeria and have been farmers in neighbouring countries for generations, operating these farms for the government. I worry about how much that empowers Nigerians in the immediate and future, given that millions of youths are unemployed. Rather than allow these young people to remain political thugs employed to perpetrate violence during elections, why don't we start a training school for farming and assist young people in farming? With that, we will be dealing with the problem of youth unemployment, we will have more food to feed our people and possibly export and ultimately improve the economy of our state, he wrote in the report he emailed to Adaora.

"Ensure that the governor gets this report, please," he said to her when he placed a call to her later that evening. "I understand you guys sit your asses on documents..."

"Wow! See hate speech," Adaora replied. They both laughed. She continued: "But seriously, don't be misguided. Civil servants may do that in some other places but not with Koras. In any case, we are not civil servants." She promised that the governor would get the email that same night. Stanley advised her that he would be informing the governor to expect the email through a text message. They wished each other a good night after agreeing to hang out the next evening.

In the days following their first hangout, Stanley and Adaora became chummy. They had discovered a mutual affection for books and the arts during his Sunday trips. During one of these moments, she had asked: "Hope you don't get too bored on these trips?"

"Not at all, I always have the company of books, you never get bored with those."

"Oh wow! You read books! Who are your favourite writers?" Adaora had queried.

Thenceforth, they had endless conversations about what and who they read, and what qualities made the best Nigerian writers.

That weekend, Stanley wrote about his experience on the back page of his paper. He commended the governor for the initiatives but pointed out all the possible pitfalls he noticed. He admonished the administration to make quick amends if the people were meant to be the ultimate beneficiaries of the projects. That same night, he got a call from the governor.

"Hello, Stanley."

"Good evening, oh morning sir."

"How are you? I saw your report and must thank you for it."

"Not at all, sir. It's a service I owe my state."

"Can you come over to the Government House to see me later today? I have a very important proposition for you."

Stanley hesitated for a few seconds and the governor noticed.

"Are you about to say no? You don't even know why I want to see you. Oh, come on, you have been there once, and you see we don't bite..."

They both laughed and that put Stanley at ease. He agreed to see the governor after his management meeting that Sunday evening.

Their meeting lasted for just ten minutes. Koras thanked the journalist for the good job he did. "I have been thinking about the lacunas you noticed in our plans and I have decided to appoint you as my Special Assistant on Special Projects."

"I am..." Stanley started, but the Governor stopped him

"Hold on, please. It's something I want you to go and think about and then come back to me. You can take two weeks. Is that fine?"

Stanley gave a feeble, almost inconspicuous nod.

"And then, I have a gift of five million naira for you. The money will be handed over to you on your way out," Koras said, extending his hands to Stanley who was too stunned and lost in thought to respond.

As much as he wanted to reject this money, he had a need for it. His mother, the only meaningful thing in his life apart from his job, which did not even pay well, was in need of a surgery that had been estimated to cost over two million naira. In addition to that, his rent would be due in two months and he had no idea where he would get that money from. He had approached the MD of his company for a loan the previous month and the man could not make any promises, he only asked that Stanley "be hopeful." He was also conscious of the suspicious looks he had been getting in the office since his return from the recent trip he took at the behest of the governor. His colleagues, most of whom were poor, beggarly, covetous and corrupt imagined that he had been paid, so why not just take the money? But then, wouldn't that run against his principles?

"Is everything okay… you want to say no? Oh, come on. You can't say no to me. I'm your governor," Koras said with a mischievous, even sardonic laughter. "Have a good night, China. I hope to hear from you in two weeks or less, right?" And the governor was gone.

On cue, Adaora walked in, a bright smile on her face.

"Hello, brainy," she said, giving a still transfixed Stanley a hug that sent waves down his body.

"What are you doing here, madam?" Stanley asked quickly recovering. He had in fact noticed his increasing affection for the beautiful Adaora. How his legs went weak and his heart beats faster anytime he was with her. That had just happened again, and he was asking himself if all these things happening to him at the same time were not some evil ploys to destroy him.

"Hello, young man, I work here, remember?"

Stanley laughed and was going to start regurgitating his conversation with the Governor when Adaora told him she knew all about it. She had the money in her car and would hand it over to him outside the car park or wherever he wanted.

"Meanwhile, let's get out of here, please."

At the car park, Stanley asked why government people walked about with so much cash. Adaora laughed and because she did not say anything, he answered his own question: "So, these monies can't be traced!"

"Oh, well. You said so. Not that we do anything illegal, but everyone is safer that way." They agreed that she should keep the money until the next day when he could put some of it in the bank.

"So, what's your plan for the rest of the evening?" Adaora asked.

"I plan to see my mother's doctor so he can arrange for a surgery that she needs urgently. What are you thinking?"

"I don't know ... just wondering ..."

"Oh yeah, I get it. Why don't I see this doctor and meet you up somewhere?"

"That would be fine."

"Okay, but where?"

"Well, come to my house, we can drive out together from there…"

"Ok then," Stanley agreed.

Adaora offered another hug, got into her car and drove off.

The following night, they had sex, twice. First, on the floor of Adaora's living room and then on her expansive bed. The sex, curiously started to do something unusual to Stanley. Driving home that night, he realised he was beginning to feel very cosy with Adaora. He had been with two girls this past year, but they were nothing near the combination of beauty, intelligence and humility that Adaora exuded. The first girl, Rosy was a co-award-winning journalist who saw her brilliance as a reason to run his life. He just could not stand her domineering; self-assured way, so they were history before their story even began. Toyin, on the other hand, was a pathetic sex-monger and leech, who thought of nothing but sex and money. They had a most regrettable relationship, which made him decide to stay off girls. Now, Adaora….

Before he left her that night, they discussed the governor's offer and Adaora advised him to waste no time in accepting it.

"You really cannot tell what other opportunities might come for you from here. More importantly, it will enhance your credentials, definitely improve your finances and as you would like to make yourself believe, you will be serving your country," she had concluded mockingly.

"What do you mean by that?" Stanley responded, feigning anger. "*I am* just interested in serving my state, nothing more, nothing less."

"I know dear. I was only pulling your long legs," she said, planting a kiss on his lips.

On getting home, Stanley sent a message to the governor confirming his willingness to take the offer. Over the next four weeks, he took a leave of absence from his job, attended to his mother's health and prepared to start work.

After two more intimate meetings with Adaora, he felt it was time to formally ask her out. They were in the restaurant of a popular hotel in the city a few days before his resumption when he broached the idea of a relationship.

Adaora stiffened in shock: "Are you serious?"

"I don't understand," Stanley said. "Isn't that just the normal order of things?"

"Oh yes, I'm surprised. It's just sex for me Stanley. I am totally surprised that you are already catching feelings."

A mixture of hurt, shock and shame congregated on Stanley's face. How could he have made such a fool of himself. He was lost for words. Adaora, guessing what might be going on in his mind offered: "Come on sweetheart, let's not get ahead of ourselves here. What I'm saying is that we should give it some time. I promise to consider it, ok?"

That was a soothing balm on Stanley's emotional bruise and an incentive for their undefined relationship to go on.

At work, Stanley proved to be an invaluable asset to the governor. Due to his understanding of development, he contributed so many ideas in the education, health and youth empowerment sectors that he soon became the right-hand man to the governor. Since his office also worked on the evaluation of projects commissioned by the government, contractors sought his favour round the clock. He found ways to avoid unnecessary patronage for the first three months in office until his journalist friends who quickly saw a difference in his lifestyle began to encourage him to make use of the office when he could. When he sought Adaora's opinion, she told him there was nothing wrong with taking gifts.

"Ensure that they complete their jobs to specification before you take anything from anyone. More importantly, it is not everyone that approaches you with gifts that you entertain, some of these guys are treacherous."

The next week a contractor who just completed a one hundred-million-naira schools renovation project walked into Stanley's office to thank him for making their job easier.

"I have worked with government for over fifteen years, and I swear the process has never been this smooth. You are such a blessing to his administration, Mr. Stanley," Mr. Odim, the contractor repeated what he had said the day before on the phone.

"I am happy to be of service to the state, sir and thank you for doing a good job."

"Oh, we are committed to delivering on our promises, my brother. After all, our people are the end users."

"True, that is what I wish every contractor would understand."

"I should be taking my leave, Oga. I know you are a busy man," Odim said, dropping a note across the table for Stanley to read.

The note asked for Stanley to give an account number where a "token of appreciation" could be sent to him. He smiled and shook his head.

"You don't have to do…"

"Oh, please, this is with all pleasure. Just oblige me, I beg," Odim pleaded with Stanley who then picked up his phone and wrote his mother's bank account number on the paper. Mr. Odim took the paper, shook hands and took his leave. Less than ten minutes later, Stanley got a bank alert for five million naira on this special vehicle account number, which he had opened in his mother's name.

Such opportunities occurred regularly and resulted in Stanley accepting them all. Sometimes, rather than take these monies himself, he told contractors to send them to the accounts of some of his journalist colleagues who always needed help. He did his best for as many of them as possible and at other times, sought the help of the governor. One of those was the MD of *The National Independent* who needed to travel abroad for a surgery. More than anyone else, however, he helped himself. By the end of his first two years in office, Stanley had already completed a mansion where he lived with his mother, who was now desperate about seeing him get married. Seeing how easy it was to get these monies without questions asked, he now had about three local accounts where contractors deposited monies for him, as well as two domiciliary accounts in United States Dollars and Great Britain Pounds. Suddenly, all became good around Stanley. He forgot the troubles of yesterday and savoured his time in the sun!

While dancing in the brightness of his growing resources however, the light went dim on his relationship with Adaora. Two things accounted for the coldness that hit their relationship. Having been in the system much longer, Adaora tried to help Stanley navigate the waters but he would have none of it. He began to see her interventions as overbearing, told her off a couple of times and eventually began to avoid her. Secondly, with more access to money came the need for a new set of friends and a change in taste for women. His new friends opened his eyes to a world of endless possibilities with girls from higher institutions in the city. So, every thought about love and settling down was pushed to the back burner, despite his mother's persistent cries. Unanswered calls and text messages from Adaora piled up on his phone just as he avoided any private meetings at the office.

Stanley was also now beginning to consider a life in politics. With the kind of resources at his disposal, he started contemplating the idea of running for office in the next elections. He was thinking about discussing the idea with Governor Koras when he received a call from the political editor of *The National Independent* one Saturday evening. The message was that a gubernatorial aspirant on the platform of another party would want to have a meeting with him. He thought his meeting with this aspirant, where he was offered the opportunity to run for office as a deputy governor was a really good one. Although he made no commitment, he promised to think about being the running mate to Chief Silas Duke, the aspirant.

He was dressing up to go to work one day when his doorbell rang. He looked at the video of the security camera and saw that it was his gateman, John.

"Yes, John, what is it?' he asked.

"Good morning, sir."

"Yes?"

"There are two men at the gate who want to see you, sir..."

"Who are they?"

"I have a card from them, sir."

"My question is who are they, can't you read the card?"

"Sorry, sir, they are from the EFCC, sir…"

"Oh! EFCC? Okay, hold on."

He walked down the stairs to the main door of the house where his gateman was waiting and took the card from him. It was a name that he knew very well as a journalist – Suleiman Aliu. He used to be one of his sources, but he couldn't fathom what this could be about. He hadn't spoken to Aliu in about three years, so this couldn't be a friendly visit. The officer would not visit him without a discussion anyways. His heart skipped a beat when it occurred to him that one of his deals might have caught up with him.

"Let them come in," he said, stepping out of the door to receive his guests.

After an exchange of pleasantries, the officers told him that he was being invited to the EFCC on the strength of a petition by a contractor who claimed to have paid him the sum of fifty million naira in lieu of the execution of a contract.

"There has not been anything like that Aliu, I swear to God," Stanley said, his voice quivering.

"Well, there is indeed a petition against you, Stanley. You will know more details when you get to the office, even you haven't been smart. I am disappointed."

"Ehn, why did you say that? What did I do?"

"You should know, and if you don't know that is even more disappointing. Ever heard the saying that he who wants to dine with the devil must bring a long spoon?

You do deals and you think the man you work for will not know? And then, you were mindless enough to start meeting with his political opponents, what got into you?"

Now, Stanley was speechless, he knew there was no point trying to deny anything. Aliu made very valid points and now, he could only pray that he hadn't played too far into the hands of the devil.

Aliu suggested that it was time to go and that out of respect for their friendship, he was going to allow Stanley drive in his car ahead of the EFCC pickup van.

"*Please* let me make a call," Stanley said to Aliu who waved him on. He dialled Adaora's number, but the phone rang out with no response. He dialled a second and third time, still no response. The same thing happened when he called Tony and John after. He consoled himself that the three personal aides of the governor might be in a meeting with their principal but deep inside, he sensed that this was a sign that he had become a persona non grata to Koras.

Tail between his legs, Stanley walked out of his home, not sure when he would be coming back. He wanted to cry but tears failed him. Yet, his heart was heavy at the mess he seemed to have made of his own reputation and how much he had become toothless in the hands of the demagogue known as Koras.

VIII
The Voice

My name is Adeza Usman. I am the only child of my mother, Hajara, and my beloved father, Ezekiel Usman, who died just after my sixteenth birthday. I remember being a very happy child. I had the total devotion of my parents, especially my father, who was in the military.

As a child, we moved around a lot. I was born in Lagos where we lived for the first seven years of my life. Then, Daddy was transferred to Benin and we moved. Daddy insisted that we move with him whenever he was transferred. I hated to change schools and say good-bye to friendships only just starting, but I loved the fact that I was never separated from my family.

For some reason that no one ever told me, my parents could not have any other child after me. As a result, Daddy felt it was sensible to have his small family with him wherever he went. So, like a snail, which goes about with its shell, we went with Dad to Benin where we stayed for four years.

Life was good in Benin City. I attended the Command Primary School, which was a stone throw away from our home and within the barracks where we lived, yet Daddy dropped me at school on his way to work every day. He also made sure he picked me up every afternoon. My mother worked in a bank on Airport Road, Benin, so she had no time to feed the endless maternal demands of an only daughter.

All through those years, Mum was out of the house at seven in the morning. They told me that she had to be at work before 7:30 a.m. and all she could do before she left for work in the morning was give me an occasional bath and then leave me with the nanny, Aunty Ada. Looking back now, I wonder why Ada always wore a stern face when she got me dressed and ready for school. She would usually mumble and grumble like a recently offended evil spirit. On occasions when I woke up feeling really grumpy, she would grudgingly lift me off my bed into the bathroom, and then snap at me.

Ada was the personification of witchcraft to me, and I rewarded her by crying a lot on days that I felt ill-spirited. The moment Ada, who was about eighteen at the time, stepped into my room I started to cry until I had a high temperature. On such days, it became my dad's duty to prepare me for school because he never wanted me to cry. I had such a great bond with my father, and he gave all that he had to his wife and only child.

I recall one occasion when my dad got in trouble with his superior at the 4th Brigade Command of the Nigerian Army in Benin. I still remember how much mother and I cried that weekend when he was said to have been locked up in a guard room for failing to make a trip with his boss to Abuja all because he dashed to pick me from school, had car trouble and did not get back in time to catch the flight on which he was supposed to travel with his commanding officer.

When Daddy dropped me at home after the car issue was fixed, a van loaded with men of the military police was parked in front of our home. A little while after we got in, someone knocked on the door and demanded that my dad follow them. I was shocked to see Daddy follow quietly like a sheep would follow its shearer. In my innocence, I ran after my dad to give him a good-bye hug, as I did when he dropped me off at home.

I began to sense trouble when one hour after Daddy was whisked away, Mum returned home wearing a most anxious look. I had been playing in my room when I heard the bell ring. Within seconds, Ada was at the door and then I heard a voice barking: "Where is Adeza?" It took me just a few seconds to realise that it was my mother and I dashed to the living room to see what the problem was.

Apparently, without waiting for Ada's reply, my mum came towards my room and we ran into each other just as I made into the living room. She held me close and broke down in tears. I was confused.

"Mummy, what is it, why are you crying? Mummy, stop crying," I said over and over again. When she would neither tell me what the problem was nor stop crying, I joined in the wailing.

That brought her back to her senses. She stood up and whispered amongst quiet sobs; "No my darling, please don't cry. Don't cry my love, everything will be okay." She held me by my right hand and led me away from the dining area to another part of the living room where we could sit comfortably. She sat me down and put my head on her laps. I waited to hear what the drama was about.

When she eventually got a hold of her emotions, she told me that Daddy had been arrested for what I now know was dereliction of duty and that he may not just be in detention for the weekend but also be on his way to losing his job if found guilty by a court martial.

Of course, all this was too much for my ten-year-old mind to comprehend, but I was paralysed by the fear that Daddy was in some risk. I was afraid that I might not see my father again and had guilt pangs for causing his travails. Since I could not do anything about the situation, I prayed that God would bring Daddy back home safely to us.

We were not allowed to visit him during that weekend. In fact, the only news we got about him was from Uncle Kelvin, his friend and course mate who was one of the top shots in the military police at the 4th Brigade.

Just before we turned in that Friday night, he visited our home and told my mum that everything was going to be alright. While Mum cried, lamenting how much she had contributed to the situation Daddy found himself in, Uncle Kelvin brought a rumpled sheet of paper out of his breast pocket and squeezed it into mum's hands. He stayed for about five minutes during which he whispered a lot of things into my mum's ear, gave each of us a goodnight hug and left.

Mercifully, Daddy came back to us on Monday evening and with the good news that his boss, Brigadier-General Falemi, who had so much liking for him had forgiven him and put an end to any further punishment. He was warned to never allow his family to infringe on his commitment to work and got no further recrimination. We were all grateful.

But we owed Gen. Falemi this gratitude for only a twinkle because less than two months after this incident, Daddy was posted to Jos, in the northern part of the country.

Things were different when we got to Jos. My dad still tried to show us love but he was more withdrawn and no longer given to much family time. In addition to that, Mum stopped working, partly because of the events of our last weeks in Benin and the fact that the bank she worked for refused to transfer her to Jos unless there was someone to replace her.

Daddy stopped being part of my early morning life, he stopped picking me up from school and we had a very short time to interact when he got back from work. I began to miss him very much.

Conversely, the sudden need for me and my mother to be together did not make me feel closer to her. Mum always complained. She would wake me up in the morning with a harsh slap on my buttocks, shout and rant all through preparations for school and grumble endlessly as I battled with my homework on return from school. It got so bad that I began to wonder if she was really my birth mother. I craved my father's attention like life itself and looked for the right opportunity to confront him about his abandonment.

The occasion presented itself when we sat down to eat breakfast one beautiful Saturday morning. I still remember well. After Daddy had blessed the meal of akara, pap and bread, which we were having, I caught him staring at me for a moment, after which he asked, a wide grin on his face and palm on my mother's hand: "Adeza, how are you this morning…?"

I barely allowed him to conclude his question before I told him that I was not fine as he did not have time for me anymore. "I miss you, Daddy," I said. Like a robot whose motion button had just been activated, he stood up from his chair at the head of the table, moved toward me, wrapped me in a tight embrace and sat on the arm of my chair.

I lifted my head to look him in the eye as he whispered: "I am sorry, my darling. It is the pressure of work and I am sure your mummy is filling in for me." He looked across the table to solicit for a consenting look from my mum who shook her head in agreement and smiled to boot. He continued: "I promise to make more time to be with you now, ok?" he planted a kiss on my cheek and moved on to finish his meal.

From then on, Daddy made every Saturday a family day. Unless work took him out of town, we stayed home on Saturdays and then after church on alternate Sundays, we ate out and visited fun places. It was a life that I would have given anything for. We had moments at the Solomon Lar Amusement Park. After hours of running round the park while my parents played board games on a particular visit, they told me it was time to go home.

I would hear nothing of the sort. When they insisted, I started to cry. I could see the embarrassment on their faces as tears rolled down my cheeks like raindrops on a windowpane, but I was not moved. Standing some distance away from them, I yelled at the top of my voice until Daddy promised that we would be visiting soon again.

I remember how I peed in my panties when I first saw a live lion at the Jos Wildlife Park, the endless bouts of boating, horse riding and eating. Life was just very good for us in Jos.

But as they say, everything, no matter how pleasurable, comes to an end. It is just that in the life of a soldier, things end so abruptly, you would want to hate life.

Just as I was about to settle into loving my life in Jos, my dad came home one day to break the news of his deployment to Sierra-Leone as part of the peace keeping mission to the troubled African country. He was to travel with the troops in two weeks and the family had to arrange how we would survive without him. That was the first time we would live apart.

The next two weeks were extremely busy for my parents. Daddy worked round the clock to be ready for his trip, prepare for the welfare of his family in his absence and bring closure to whatever his duties at the 3rd Armoured Division were.

From conversations with my mum, I understood that army authorities would allow us stay in the three -bedroom apartment that we occupied at the Rukuba Cantonment for as long as Daddy was away, and that I could go on with school in Jos. I was also told that my dad would be away for one year and that there were possibilities that he would be able to make it down to visit us once or twice in the duration of his foreign deployment.

It turned out that Daddy spent three years in this service during which he visited us only three times. It was the period that I needed my father most, but we were only able to communicate through emails and occasional telephone calls. Daddy had insisted that I have a phone few months after he travelled, although he battled with my mum over this for several months. For reasons that I still do not get, my mum cut me no slack when it came to stuff that could give me a measure of comfort. But, due to Daddy's insistence, I got a phone when he visited at the end of his first year on the mission.

On each of the occasions that he came home, he spent about two weeks of which we had very limited time together. Senior secondary school was more serious work than anything I had imagined, and I stayed back at school to take extra lessons until about 5 p.m. every weekday.

But we spent quality time together on weekends. Daddy would tell us about the country where he was working, the suffering of the people and how he prayed that war and strife would never happen in Nigeria again.

We talked about my education, he asked me about my childhood desire to be a lawyer, whether I still wanted that and how seriously I took my literature and history, two subjects that he was very good in. We would gist about my friends. I told him I had only one, Grace, whose father was a top lawyer at the Plateau State Ministry of Justice. Daddy asked me to invite her home on his next visit.

Then he teased me about boys. One conversation my mum never wanted him to have with me, but Daddy always found his way. He would sneak into my room when Mum was in the kitchen or otherwise engaged, asking questions about what his "adorable daughter was doing with the boys".

I always looked at him smiling away after telling him I was not interested in boys yet, he would advise: "I just want the best for you, my princess. You know you mean the world to your mum and I, so please do not disappoint us. I want you to face your studies for now but even if you are thinking of having any boyfriend, you should be free to talk to us about it," he would say and usually give me a peck on the cheek before letting himself out of my room as quietly as he had stolen in. I could never forget the tenderness with which Daddy attended to anything that concerned me. He was a father in six billion!

Three years flew past before we realised it. During this period, I had sat for my school certificate examinations and passed it in flying colours. I also did well in the university matriculation examination and was offered admission to study Law at the University of Jos. This gladdened the hearts of my parents as we all awaited my matriculation at the beginning of the next academic session. We all agreed that Daddy was going to seek the permission of his superiors to attend. And then providence stepped in!

Three months before the day set for my matriculation, I received Daddy's email that he was coming back home. I was beside myself with joy. It was a very simple email that I still read over in my mind every now and then. It goes as follows:

Guess what, my Princess? Daddy is coming back home. The army headquarters and the UN just sent signals that we are returning home. It is the end of our mission!

For the next one week, my mum and I ran all over the city of Jos preparing for the return of our champion. We cleaned the house and planned a surprise welcome party to which all of our family friends were invited.

The flight that brought him and 200 hundred other soldiers back landed in Lagos at about twelve noon on the set date. It was a Saturday. He immediately called to tell us that they had landed, explained that sorting out their luggage might take the rest of the day and that he would pass the night with his classmate at the Ikeja cantonment.

On Sunday afternoon, he flew to Abuja where he would stay for the next five days. Every day, he called to tell us the progress that was made in the series of debriefing sessions at the army headquarters. This went on until Friday evening when the exercise was concluded. Finally, Daddy was coming back home on Saturday!

I woke up early on the D-day. At about 7 a.m., I knocked on my mum's door to find out if she was awake. She was. She told me she could not sleep much at night and tried to rouse Daddy up from sleep, just for them to gist. But his phone did not connect.

We decided to wait another hour before calling him. Although he was an early riser, we reasoned that the last few days had been really eventful, and he deserved to rest. We never made that call.

A few minutes before 8 a.m., we heard a knock on our door. My mum and I glanced at each other. I wondered whether Daddy had pulled a fast one on us. Simultaneously, we asked: "Who is that?" There was no reply for what looked like an eternity and then we heard the voice of one of Daddy's junior colleagues and friend,

Major Chris, saying: "It is Chris." Again, my mum and I stared at each other and then she said: "Maybe he is with your daddy."

Mummy grabbed a wrapper, tied it around her and like excited children who just sighted their favourite candy, we both made for the door to receive Major Chris and whoever may be accompanying him.

The story was half told as soon as my mum unlatched the door to see not just Uncle Chris but Brigadier-Gen Samah who was the Commandant of the 3rd Division. Their faces wore a look that communicated the gloom of the situation to us than any spoken word could. And in the tradition of the military, the presence of Brig Samah at our doorsteps at that time of the day told the finality of the situation to my mum.

The import of the situation did not dawn on me until my mum yelled: "What happened, ehn? What happened, where is Ezekiel?" At this moment, the commandant's wife, in the company of a number of other ladies in the cantonment, stepped out of a waiting vehicle and moved close to my mum. They held her as she wailed, asking why her husband of close to twenty years would leave her this way. It was a very emotional moment in which I was surprisingly stoic. It was not until after the seventh day, that we had the presence of mind to ask questions about what exactly happened to the good soldier, Ezekiel Usman.

Unknown to us, Daddy and two of his Jos-based colleagues with whom he served on the mission decided to surprise their families by arriving Jos on Friday night. So, at 7 p.m., they left Abuja in a Peugeot 406 belonging to one of these other officers for the three-hour journey to Jos. It was the last journey they were ever going to make.

Just one hour before they got to Jos, their car ran into a stationary fuel tanker that had broken down and had been left in the middle of the road without any sign of caution to oncoming vehicles.

Eyewitnesses told military and police authorities that the car they travelled in burst into flames on impact against the tanker and the whole village was engulfed in a fire that razed countless thatched houses, leaving in its trail a flow of sorrow, tears and blood. It was a disaster of monumental propositions for this otherwise peaceful village, ten kilometres from Barkin Ladi, a disaster, which officially ended my life.

There was no way to recover from the untimely death of Daddy. He was the only friend I had, the one who listened to me. The one who taught me things I knew as a baby, things I would never forget, the only one who spoke to my heart.

Life changed significantly for me after Daddy passed on. Of course, Mum and I now only had one another, and we tried to make the best of this reality, even if for a fleeting moment. She and those who sympathise with her have not stopped blaming me for ruining our relationship because I refused to get over my father's death. But they do not understand that all their complaints and everything that has happened after Daddy's passage only make me feel a stronger need to be with him. It is the failure to understand that that has brought us to the current place we find ourselves in. Let me tell you the story.

Against my wishes, Mum succeeded in forcing me to resume at the University of Jos three months after our loss. It did not make sense to me. Although, I had always wanted to get an education and become a lawyer, that urge mostly came from a desire to make Daddy happy and truth be told, the desire died with him.

I went to the university as she wanted but learnt nothing. I kept to myself in class without a wish to learn anything. In fact, the only thing I did in class was relive the time I spent with my daddy.

Every day, I got back home and locked myself up in my room, refusing to engage in any serious conversation with mum. Even when she came to seek me out, I rebuffed her, I just wanted to be by myself.

With the way I behaved at home, Mum realised that things must be bad at school. She visited my school without informing me and was told that I was not doing well at all. So, when I got home that evening, she had prepared some pep talk that led us nowhere. I told her in plain terms that she was the one who forced me to go to school and should therefore bear the consequences.

While my mother battled with the frustration of my inability to concentrate in class and the constant talk about the urge to join Daddy wherever he was, the Nigerian

Army served us a notice to quit our accommodation in the barracks. This was in spite of the fact that the authorities were yet to pay his entitlement for the twenty years of meritorious service he gave his country.

For some months, we lived with one of his very close friends in the barracks after which my mum secured a modest two-bedroom apartment in the Government Reservation Area.

But before we moved out, someone introduced my mum to a spiritualist. I got to know this one Saturday morning, when she asked me to go out with her on a brief visit to someone. I reluctantly agreed, only to realise that I had been the object of her visit to this man. He spoke about the need to exorcise some spirits of the dead that tortured me. That was the last day I went anywhere with my mother.

I spent three years in school before I was advised to withdraw. The desire to live had totally left me. I was in a dark place and the only thought I had was to be with the only one who understood me – Daddy – again. I constantly heard a voice in my head telling me of how I could help myself achieve that and on one or two occasions, I contemplated suicide.

I frequently saw Daddy in my dreams, he would smile at me and wave his hands like it was impossible for us to see again. I would cry my eyes out in the dream and remain in my room for days after. Mum didn't know what to do with me.

Then, one strange man started to appear in our home. That was not something I bargained for. Each time he came, I would hear him and mum giggle like babies. It was a spectacle I hated, one which made me to want to end it all as quickly as possible. Sometimes we sat on the table together to eat but I hardly spoke to him beyond the good mornings and good afternoons that tradition imposed on me.

One afternoon, I overheard a conversation between this man and my mum. He complained about the way I behaved and how worried he was that she kept me at home without seeking help. Mum informed him about the intervention of the spiritualist and how that had made me even more reclusive.

He then told my mum: "I think she needs to see a doctor. I suspect that she has a medical condition which should be treated before it gets out of hand. I am going to talk to a consultant friend at the teaching hospital and see how he can help."

This really infuriated me. I felt like rushing out and giving him a piece of my mind but then, the voice in my head calmed me down, telling me: *shh, don't be so hasty, there will be a better opportunity to deal with this man, so just keep your cool*. I smiled at the reassurance with the contentment of a babe suckling at the breast of a doting mother. It was my first smile in a long, long while.

That same night, I had a dream. I saw Daddy. Again, I made an effort to rush to him but a man whose face I couldn't see stood solidly in my way. I cried! I struggled with the strange figure, but he was far too strong for me.

And then, it all fell in place in the morning. The voice in my head, my only friend in the past two years, told me that the man I saw in my dream was my mum's new friend. *And we must find a way to end his attempt to stop you from reuniting with your dad*, my friend told me. That day, we discussed a number of ways to deal with this man. We finally found a way and I was happy!

Some days after, I heard the door to our home open at about four in the afternoon. Sure, that it was my mother's wicked friend, I moved close to the door of my room so I would know the perfect time to execute the plan.

From their conversation, I learnt that mum and this man were going to visit his doctor friend on my behalf, something which the voice immediately told me was fatal to my ambition. When mum stepped out of the living room to conclude preparations for their outing, I tiptoed out of my room, my right hand behind me with the object of my mission tucked in. I snuck in behind the chair where the enemy of my soul was seated and stuck the knife in my hand into his left back side with all the energy I could muster.

Done, I dropped the knife and fled into my room just as my mum rushed out on hearing what I hoped was the dying scream of her wicked lover boy. I do not know how he was rushed out of the house to the hospital, not that I care though. What saddens me is that I failed in my mission. I am angry that doctors were able to save his life. I am angry at the irony that this life is. A good man like my father dies, without a trace of his body, yet a wicked soul like my mum's friend is saved. How more cruel and unfair could life be?

I was soon taken out of the house by policemen, first locked up in some cell and then moved to something they call a mental home, where they claim I will get some healing. But that means nothing to me, nothing is as important to me as being with Daddy again, and I know that will happen one day soon, my friend and I are planning to make it happen.

When it happens, they will tell you all sorts about me, so I had to tell you my story, just to let you know that I am not the bad person, those who stop me from being with my father again, those who are against my soul should take all the blame for this.

IX
The Drive

"***Good afternoon, lady, which way are you headed?***"

Startled, Yemisi looked up from her phone. She was surprised to see a car coming to a stop just in front of her. She was trying to reply a message from Ade who is best friends with Tosin, her boyfriend of two years until last night. She had been too engrossed in contemplating a fitting response to his message to notice the Honda Civic car drive past or come back and level up to the point where the driver could speak directly to her. She was at a loss on how to respond to the intruder's question. After gaping for about thirty seconds, she spoke up.

"Hmm, good afternoon, please don't..." she stopped short of rejecting the offer of the well-shaven guy at the wheels of the car when she thought about how long she had been in the bite of that afternoon's scorching sun. Checking the time on her phone, she noticed that it had been twenty-three minutes since she alighted from the Uber that took her from home in fury.

Thinking about it again now, she wondered what could have been troubling the guy and blamed herself for not driving out in her own car. Now, she wanted to have someone drive her so she could think straight and discover where she had gone wrong with Tosin and now, this crazy Uber guy!

All she said to him was to please reduce the speed at which he was travelling, but the Franklin guy spat anger at her like a cobra would venom. He went from ranting about how every little prostitute looked down on Uber drivers to how he had had enough of the nagging of women. Yemisi was shocked at the sudden eruption and every time she made to ask what the trouble was, Franklin's tempo rose so that she had no choice than to ask him to drop her off by the roadside. She noticed that the driver took a quick look at the mirror, pulled off the road and told her to "get off."

"Can you end the trip, so I'll know what to pay for the distance you have covered?" Yemisi said to the driver still trying to play fair.

But cab man was not in the mood to have her company for another second. He seemed so totally disgusted with her that he blurted out: "Please get out of my car this second before I force you out!" At this point, Yemisi knew she was dealing with a relentlessly angry man and that the situation could become really ugly if she did not leave the vehicle as fast as her legs could carry her. As she made to pick her small travel bag from the back seat, she could hear the hard breathing of her driver as clearly as the sound of a saw cutting wood. She opened the car door, picked her bag and dashed out of the car just as Franklin zoomed off like a rocket.

"Hello," the stranger offering the ride disrupted Yemisi's thoughts, startling her again.

"Oh, I am sorry. I am heading to Lekki Phase 1, are you going in that direction?" she asked the stranger, looking from his face to the back of the car as if to assure herself that she would be safe in his company. "Even if that isn't your way, I'll appreciate it if you can get me close to Ogudu, where I can get a taxi because…"

"It's fine, please come in. Luckily for us both, I am going your way," the guy in the car responded. He beckoned on her to come into the car and stretched across the passenger seat to open the door just about the same time she did. Their eyes locked in a fleeting embarrassing look, followed by an uncomfortable smile, at least for Yemisi.

They were getting onto the Third Mainland Bridge before either of them broke the uncomfortable silence in the vehicle, and when it happened, it was Yemisi who thanked her benefactor for his kindness.

"But what were you doing at that spot this hot afternoon? You stay around there or something?" The man asked, adding almost instinctively, "Forgive me, for not being gentlemanly, my name is David, what is yours?"

Yemisi, offering a vulnerable smile replied, "I am Yemisi, and thank you again for being so kind…" The smile on her face gradually paled into a worrisome look as the thought of stories of free rides turned nightmares crept into her mind.

"Really nice to meet you," David said, cutting into her thought. "So, I asked what you were doing there," he continued.

Yemisi forced a smile before starting the story of her ordeal with the Uber driver and her efforts to order another ride before he arrived on the scene. As she concluded her story, Yemisi said a little prayer in her heart that this ride would end well for her.

"Wow," David said laughing. "There are so many angry people walking the streets these days, mehn. One just needs to be careful. I hope he doesn't end up hurting someone or even himself…"

"Exactly! That was the fear I had o," Yemisi interrupted, throwing her hands up in a gesture of helplessness. "But the guy would not even let me speak, I wonder what problems he could have been dealing with…"

"Anyways, let's wish your angry driver the best," David said with a mischievous smile. "So, do you stay in Lekki, or what is happening there?" he continued, taking his eyes off the steering wheel momentarily to take a look at her. She had a glossy brown skin, which glowed under a quarter-sleeved shirt and short denim skirt. Her eyes, under well-decorated eyebrows, were dreamy, the kind in which a man could see tomorrow.

"I am going to see my friend, she stays at Lekki Phase 1," Yemisi replied.

"Oh, I see. And you are going to be there for a while, I see you have a packed bag."

"Yes, I will be in Lekki for a couple of days," Yemisi said. She remembered that her response to Ade's message was pending. She asked David to give her a moment to reply the message and then went on to fish the phone out of her bag.

Yes, I will be at Linda's house this weekend but see, Ade, I really don't think there is anything to discuss concerning this matter. It just cannot work between Tosin and I. I think I have done my best, even though I truly appreciate your support, she typed on her phone, sent the message and shook her head vigorously. She browsed through her phone and noticed that she had received twenty missed calls from Tosin in the period that she got into David's car. Tears welled up in her eyes as she remembered the pains she has had to deal with in the last twenty-four hours. It was like her whole world had come crashing down and she couldn't even tell where to pick it up from again.

She met Tosin shortly after she broke things up with Nnamdi, the Igbo guy she was in love with for four years. She met Nnamdi in her second year at the University of Lagos when he visited her roommate, Ifeyinwa, who was his cousin. He was an elegant piece of work that everyone, male or female took a second look at.

The first attraction for Yemisi was his cologne, it had a smooth masculinity that would leave a seductive impact on any girl. And then, Nnamdi was a great communicator. He spoke impeccable English, and as they spent more time together, she discovered that she hadn't met anyone with as wide a vocabulary of the English language as he. Over and above everything, he was very thoughtful.

He apparently spotted and took interest in her on his first visit and by the time he was visiting again, he had a bag full of gifts for Yemisi. Before long, the two of them became inseparable, even looking forward to a future together.

But while it was Yemisi's legitimate right to propose, the ultimate right of disposal lay with her father. The day Mr. Adekoye learnt that his daughter was in a relationship with an Igbo boy was the beginning of the end of that delightful affair. Try as she did, her father refused to bless the union, so they went their separate ways.

Enter Tosin. Nowhere near Nnamdi in any of the departments, but he was at least a Yoruba boy. Tosin had a very unstable, if you like, flirtatious temper, dictated by the person he was dealing with.

Although he worked as a bank manager in another branch of Omega Bank where Yemisi also worked, it was possible to count how many times her boyfriend ever bought her or anyone around her a gift. It didn't matter whether it was any one's birthday or Valentine's Day, Tosin was one of those guys whose only incentive was a profit in sight. But none of these tendencies, which Yemisi repeatedly brought to her parents' notice made any sense to them. Not even her complaints about his frequent dalliances with other women, which Yemisi had become privy to made them imagine Tosin out of the life of their twenty-eight-year-old daughter.

Unrepentant in her belief that sunset arrives early for girls, Yemisi's retired teacher mother would always tell her, "Don't let this young man slip out of your hands, time is of the essence, my dear daughter."

So, Yemisi, not willing to go against the wishes of her parents chose to subordinate her preferences and throw herself into the relationship with Tosin. She endured every and anything he brought her way and sacrificed everything she had, including her body and finances to make the man of her life happy. As they began to talk about marriage, Tosin began to make consistent financial demands on Yemisi. Just the previous month, he had spoken about some investment that would yield a two-hundred-percent interest in one month.

"See, baby, these returns are guaranteed and there would be no story, I swear," he told Yemisi that rainy evening he drove to her house after work.

"Hmm," Yemisi pondered and finally said, "You know I have no objections to investments but there is the issue of the one million you took two months ago, which you have not returned. Now, you want another million, when we have the wedding ahead of us."

After a lot of back and forth, he promised that the total sum of two million naira would be returned after one month and that they would then speed up preparations for their wedding. The next morning, Yemisi transferred one million naira to him, hoping that the money would return to her in another four weeks.

But what she got four weeks later hit her for six. She had just stepped out of the shower after a very eventful day at work when her phone rang. She ran towards the bed where she left the phone and took the call just before it finally rang out.

"Hello, is that Yemisi?" an urgent female voice queried.

"Hello, yes, this is she. Who am I speaking with, please?"

"My name is Philomena, and I am calling just to advise you. I understand that you are in a relationship with Tosin Ajanla and thought I should let you know that you are just wasting your time. I am three months pregnant for this man and we are in fact, getting married in a couple of months. I hope you will have the sense to take my advice. Have a good evening." The phone clicked.

Yemisi looked on at her phone unable to say a word. She could not remember ever being so stupefied in her entire life. Thoughts rang through her mind as to what to do next. Call Linda, her best friend, call her mum, or call Tosin, the devil himself. "But why am I calling him the devil, when I have not even confirmed anything that this scammer said? Imagine me! I actually should call Tosin and make him laugh at this prank," she said smiling, a sense of relief sweeping over her.

While trying to dial Tosin's number, she got a WhatsApp message from an unknown number. With shaking hands, she terminated the call and opened the message to see her Tosin in the arms of a lady she could not recognise.

"Look, Philo, this is the most exciting day of my life. I have always told you that once pregnancy happens, we are getting married," Tosin started and got off the bed to pick up his shirt from the wardrobe.

Yemisi stopped the video and forwarded the two-minute recording to Tosin's phone. She noticed that he was online and opened the video immediately. Within two minutes, Yemisi's phone rang, it was him.

"What is this about, Tosin, is this true?" she asked.

"Listen, baby, I c....an e...x...plain," he stuttered.

"No, just answer my question. Do you know that woman and is she pregnant with your baby? Just fucking answer me!"

"Emm..."

"So, it is true," Yemisi interjected.

"Yes, it is, but it is not what you think..."

"God punish you, Tosin, and please, don't even try to call me. Go after the woman having your baby..." Yemisi ended the call, dropped her phone on the floor and crashed on the bed wailing.

After lying in that position for about two hours, she called her friend Linda who offered to come over even though it was late but Yemisi promised that she would be fine. She promised to come over to see her friend instead and spend a few days "to rethink my life".

Before daybreak, Yemisi had received about one hundred calls from five of their mutual friends but she was not in the mood to speak with anyone.

David looked to his side and noticed that the lady beside him was in tears. "Oh my God, are you okay?" He said, stretching out his right hand to hold and comfort Yemisi.

In the same instant, he looked up and saw that he was one foot away from a stationary PSP waste disposal truck. He slammed on the brakes as hard as he could, but rather than come to a halt, the car flew into the air, landed once and went up again. By the time the car came to a final halt near the layby that leads to Ikoyi, it had somersaulted three times, flinging its driver out of the car onto a gorge on the right side of the road.

"Ah, *iyen ti ku*, that one is dead, no debate," one of the five area boys always loitering the area declared. They swarmed around the car to see what they could pilfer before law enforcement arrived.

Yemisi made an effort to open her eyes, a first, second and third time. Her eyelids suddenly became too heavy, falling on their own volition until they took a final bow and closed eternally. The boys around paid no attention to the lady. While two of them watched out for any signs of policemen, three ransacked what remained of the car. They went for the travel bag at the back and stripped her motionless body of her wristwatch and gold necklace. As they made to leave, they heard the ringing of a phone. Two of them ran back to the car, found the ringing phone. The name of the caller was Linda.

"*Gbe phone yen, ko so fun pe eni to n pe ti ku*," the one who seemed to be more elderly of the five shouted at his colleague.

"Hello, Yemisi, how far now?" Linda said.

"Hey, hey, this is not Yemisi. Your friend is dead o. She had an accident around Adeniji, you better come find her." He hung up, switched off the phone and went to join his accomplices who were already rejoicing over the harvest of that day.

About the Author

Niran Adedokun is a public relations practitioner, lawyer and writer. He is the author of *Ladies Calling the Shots*, a profile of seventeen top female film and television directors in Nigeria, released in 2017 and *The Danfo Driver in All of Us and Other Essays,* a compilation of his reflections on national issues, published over a period of eight years. Adedokun is also a columnist with The PUNCH and TheCable.ng newspapers. *The Law is an Ass* is his first work of fiction.